Drug Lords Of The World

Dr Binoy Gupta

Ukiyoto Publishing

All global publishing rights are held by

Ukiyoto Publishing

Published in 2023

Content Copyright © Dr Binoy Gupta

ISBN 9789360162535

All rights reserved.
No part of this publication may be reproduced, transmitted, or stored in a retrieval system, in any form by any means, electronic, mechanical, photocopying, recording or otherwise, without the prior permission of the publisher.

The moral rights of the author have been asserted.

This book is sold subject to the condition that it shall not by way of trade or otherwise, be lent, resold, hired out or otherwise circulated, without the publisher's prior consent, in any form of binding or cover other than that in which it is published.

www.ukiyoto.com

Contents

Introduction	1
Alcohol & Al Capone	5
The Golden Triangle	24
Tse Chi Lop Asia-Pacific's Biggest Drug Lord	38
The Golden Crescent	52
The Medellin And The Cali Drug Cartels	57
Mexican Drug Cartels	74
Joaquín El Chapo Guzman	93
Druglords Of Brazil	100
Drug Lords Of India	114
About the Author	*119*

Introduction

Drug Lords and Cartels have always fascinated me. They are almost like parallel Governments – run professionally, but far more ruthlessly. It all started with Alcohol and prohibition.

Alcohol and narcotics are addictive or habit forming drugs. These have been used for medicinal purposes for centuries. They were used for addiction, but in insignificant quantities. In modern times, addiction to them has become a source of major concern to most countries, far more to the developed ones.

The illegal traffic in narcotic drugs generates huge amounts of money. This money is used to bribe, corrupt, threaten and even kill politicians and government officials. This has given rise to drug lords like Al Capone, Khun Sa, Chao Nyi Lai, Bao Youxiang, Lao Ta Saenlee, Wei Hsueh-kang, Hajji Bashir Noorzai of Afghanistan, General Noriega, Pablo Escobar, Griselda Blanco the Queenpin, Félix Gallardo of Mexico, Joaquín El Chapo Guzman, Ng Sik-ho, Tse Chi Lop and many others. They have also created drug cartels like the Medellin and Cali Cartels, Sinaloa Cartel. Brazil has entered the field rather late. The drug lords are filthy rich, totally ruthless and wield enormous power. They can get any one - including the police, military and the judiciary - attacked and killed.

At the same time, since the fight against narcotic drugs is being tackled at the International levels, a large portion of the illegal money has to be laundered to hide the source of money creating innumerable problems necessitating ingenious solutions.

Many of the Drug Lords have cultivated a Robin Hood type of image often helping the poor and needy. Their stories have been converted into block buster movies and TV serials. Best seller books have been written about them.

The developed countries are spending huge sums of money and resources to fight the menace – to stop production of various drugs;

to catch and punish the producers, distributors and retailers; and to treat and rehabilitate the habituated. The fight against narcotic drugs is one of the foremost social priorities in such countries as the U.S. and Europe.

India is not lagging behind. The seizure, and therefore the import of drugs into India, have increased manifold over the recent years. Drugs have become a serious problem. And this requires far more and far greater efforts for stopping the trade, catching and punishing the guilty and treating the addicted.

On 15 September 2021, the Directorate of Revenue Intelligence (DRI), India seized two containers at Mundra Port in Gujarat on the basis of secret intelligence information that they contained narcotics. The containers had originated from Afghanistan after takeover of the country by the Taliban on 15 August 2021. The cargo had been shipped from Bandar Abbas Port in Iran to Mundra Port, Gujarat. The cargo had been declared as semi-processed talc stones from Afghanistan. The containers had been imported by a firm in Vijayawada in Andhra Pradesh. The narcotics were headed towards New Delhi. Two persons were arrested in connection with the seizure. Investigations were taken over by the National Investigation Agency (NIA) and are in progress.

The DRI officials recovered 2,988 kg (6,590 pounds) of heroin worth an estimated Rs. 21,000 crores. This is the biggest haul of narcotics in India to date. It is not known whether this was the first consignment or more had entered through the port earlier.

The Opium Poppy has been cultivated in India at least since the 15th century. When the Mughal Empire was on the decline, the British East India Company assumed monopoly over the cultivation of opium poppy. By 1873, the entire trade was brought under government control.

After India gained independence, the cultivation and trade of opium passed on to the Indian government. The activity was controlled by The Opium Act, 1857, The Opium Act, 1878, and The Dangerous Drugs Act, 1930. At present, the cultivation and processing of poppy and opium is controlled by the provisions of The Narcotic Drugs and Psychotropic Substances (NDPS) Act and Rules.

Due to the potential for illicit trade and risk of addiction, cultivation of opium poppy is strictly regulated in India. The crop is allowed to be sown only in tracts of land notified by the central government in 22 districts in the states of Madhya Pradesh, Uttar Pradesh, and Rajasthan.

The cultivation of opium poppy is strictly monitored by the government through satellite images to check for illicit cultivation. Once the crop is ready, the Government officials have a formula on how much the yield should be. This entire quantity is then purchased by the government and processed entirely at the Government Opium and Alkaloid Factories in Ghazipur, Uttar Pradesh and Neemuch, Madhya Pradesh. Morphine, codeine, thebaine, and oxycodone are produced from the opium poppy. Despite being one of the few global cultivators of poppy, India still imports these active pharmaceutical ingredients as well as poppy seeds, which is also consumed as a food item in the country.

India has opened up the highly regulated sector of producing and processing opium to private players. Under a trial phase, Bajaj Healthcare Ltd. based in Thane, Maharashtra is the first company to win tenders for producing concentrated poppy straw that is used to derive alkaloids that are the active pharmaceutical ingredient in pain medication and cough syrups. The Government will provide the poppy straw. Bajaj Healthcare Ltd. will process 6,000 MT of unopened poppy capsules and opium gum in its factory in Savli, near Vadodara to produce active pharmaceutical ingredients over the next five years. On 23 November, 2022, Bajaj Healthcare Limited announced the inauguration of new production line for Processing of Opium at Savli, Gujarat, India and commencement of the trial run for the same.

The government has roped in the private sector to boost the domestic production of various alkaloids such as morphine and codeine which are still imported. This would also mean reduction in imports. The move is also aimed at offsetting the declining area under cultivation of poppy in India in 2017 and 2019. This could be Rs. 1000 crore business with more future potential.

In this small book, I have written about alcohol and different addictive drugs; given a brief idea of some of the biggest drug lords and drug cartels; mentioned

the efforts made at the International levels to curb trafficking in drugs and touched the narcotic laws with reference to India.

Dr Binoy Gupta

Alcohol & Al Capone

Alcohol is the oldest and most widely used addictive drug. Today alcohol is used in almost all festivities in the Western world. The reason for its wide use is its ease of production. When any sugary juice, including the juice of fruits, is left in warm air for a few days, yeasts which are present in the atmosphere, ferment it into alcoholic beverage.

Man also learnt that when starchy cereals, like maize, were chewed and spit into water, the amylase present in the saliva converted the starch into sugar, and yeasts in the atmosphere fermented the sugar into alcohol.

The Chinese were making a kind of wine from rice, honey, and fruit 9,000 years ago. We find details of the use of alcoholic beverages, and the consequences of habitual intoxication in our own 'Ayurveda', written 5000 years ago. We find prescriptions for preparing beer written by Sumerian physicians on clay tablets almost 4000 years ago. In India *toddy* or palm wine is quite common all over the country. It is taken as either neera or patanīr (a sweet, non-alcoholic beverage derived from fresh sap), or kallu (a sour beverage made from fermented sap. The alcoholic content in the fermented beverage is between 3% to 6% - about the strength of beer, but not as strong as wine.

The process of fermentation by which sugars are converted into alcohol and carbon dioxide continues only till the sugar content is exhausted or until the level of alcohol reaches 14% by volume. Once this concentration is reached, the yeasts cannot survive, and fermentation stops.

Around 800 B.C., an Arab Jabir Ibn Hayyan (Born: c. 721 Died: c. 815) developed the art of distillation. Thereafter, it became possible to prepare more concentrated and potent alcoholic drinks. Country Liquor or Indian-made Indian liquor (IMIL) or Desi daroo is a category of liquor made in the countryside of the Indian subcontinent. It is fermented and distilled from molasses, a bye product of sugarcane. They are traditionally prepared by a procedure that has been passed down for centuries. Due to cheap prices, country liquor is the most popular alcoholic beverage among the impoverished people. It includes both legally and illegally made local alcohol.

It is estimated that nearly two-thirds of the alcohol consumed in India is country liquor. Since country liquor is cheaper than other spirits, there are reports of mixing country liquor with Scotch/English whisky in many bars in India.

If care is not taken in the distillation process and proper equipment is not used, harmful impurities such as fusel alcohols, lead from plumbing solder, and methanol rise to toxic levels. Several deaths are reported in India due to consumption of non-factory made toxic liquor.

The State of Goa, India has its own indigenous alcoholic liquor Feni (also called fenno or fenny). The two most popular types of feni are Cashew Feni and Coconut Feni, depending on the ingredients used in distillation. However, several other varieties and newer blends are available. Feni is rather strong having alcoholic content between 42% to 45% by volume.

History shows that almost every society tolerates at least one addictive drug

The same society despises drugs tolerated by other societies. Mexican Indians strongly detested alcohol. The punishment for appearing in a public place in a drunken state was death. But the same Mexicans tolerated the far more potent hallucigen mescaline. Most Muslim cultures have forbidden the use of alcohol, but they do not find the use of cannabis and opium objectionable.

Alcohol became the chosen intoxicant of Europe and of other countries influenced by European culture. Alcohol came to be associated with every function, every celebration – Christmas, New Year, Easter, birthdays and funerals, marriages and anniversaries. Every moment of happiness had to be accompanied by drinks and every moment of sorrow had to be drowned in drinks.

By the eighteenth century, the increasing abuse of alcohol started giving rise to alarm in different quarters in various countries. We will now move to the U.S.

Rise and Fall of Gangs in U.S.

The great gangs of U.S. were born in the 1820s and continued till the end of World War I. They operated in two major fields: -
   i) Committing violent crimes; and
   ii) Acting as bully boys of political machines in the big cities.
By 1914, these violent gangs had been almost wiped out.

Introduction of Prohibition in U.S. - the Volstead Act of 1919
After the end of the First World War in November 2018, the problem of alcohol became so acute that Americans started clamouring for prohibition. Some states were 'dry' but the Supreme Court ruled that the Congress had exclusive power to regulate interstate transport. Therefore, any one could bring liquor from a neighbouring 'wet' state and sell it in the 'dry' state, provided he did not change its original packing and label. This led to the Eighteenth Amendment to the Constitution and the enactment of the National Prohibition Act (commonly known as the Volstead Act) in 1919. The Volstead Act which came into effect from 1920 prohibited the manufacture, transport and sale of intoxicating liquors which were defined as any liquid which contained more that 0.5% intoxicant by volume. The Volstead Act specified that "no person shall manufacture, sell, barter, transport, import, export, deliver, furnish or possess any intoxicating liquor except as authorized by this act" but it did not specifically prohibit the purchase or consumption of intoxicating liquors.

Chicago Gangsters - Alphonse Gabriel Capone

Chicago, too, had its share of criminal gangs. The most famous of the Chicago gang leaders was Alphonse Gabriel Capone, commonly known as Al 'Scarface' Capone. From 1925 to 1929, after Al Capone relocated to Chicago, he enjoyed the status of the most notorious mobster in the country. He cultivated a certain image of himself in the public that made him a subject of fascination. He wore custom made suits, smoked expensive cigars, savoured gourmet food and drinks, and enjoyed female company. He was particularly known for his flamboyant and costly jewellery. Al Capone remains one of the most notorious gangsters of the 20th century. He has been the subject of numerous books, articles, TV serials and films. Several successive mobsters have tried to emulate him.

Al Capone earned the appendage 'Scarface' to his name from the huge scar on his left face inflicted with a knife by a toughee Frank Gallucio during an altercation over a girl. Al Capone often claimed that he received the scar injury during military duty. The fact is he never was in the military. And surprising as this may appear, in later years, Al Capone appointed Gallucio his personal bodyguard.

Mafia

Contrary to popular belief, Al Capone was not connected with the Mafia. The word Mafia, stands for *Morte Alla Francia Italia Anela* (meaning in Italian *Death to France is Italy's Cry*). The acronym Mafia was devised for a secret society which was formed in Sicily in the 1860s to combat the French forces which were threatening the freedom of Italy. Later, the society became less concerned with patriotism, and more with power and money. Mafia was organized into families under strict disciplinary control of their leaders. They took an oath of silence, breach of which was punished with death. Mussolini almost finished them off in the 1930s. But they helped U.S. forces invade Sicily in 1943, and U.S. gave them a fresh lease of life. The word Mafia is now commonly used for organized criminals. Al Capone was not a Sicilian, but an Italian. In reality, he spent his entire life quarreling with the Mafia.

Al Capone was born in Brooklyn in 1899. He attended school till the sixth grade when he beat up his female teacher. In turn, he was beaten up by the principal and quit school. He started career as a dish washer. At an early age, he joined the James Street Gang, a subsidiary of the Five Points Gang – a larger gang headed by another Italian, John Torro, which later Al Capone joined. When he was only 15, Al Capone learnt that a Mafia gang was extorting money from his father. Al Capone shot dead the two persons responsible.

With the introduction of prohibition through the enactment of the Volstead Act in 1920, production and distribution of illicit liquor became big business. All the gangs seized the new opportunity and entered the business of illicit liquor.

The Prohibition Agents – U.S.

The Federal Government recruited 1500 Prohibition Agents – officials who were to enforce the Volstead Act. Most of these agents were poorly qualified and their wages were a measly $ 200 a month. They were despised by the gangsters as well as by the public. The local police also hated them because they had been thrust upon them by the Federal Government.

The word 'Prohibition Agent' became a bye word for corruption. Many prohibition agents maintained lavish life styles moving about in flashy cars with girls at their sides. Between 1920 and 1928, the Treasury Department dismissed 706 prohibition agents for larceny. Captain Dan Chaplin, then Chief of New York Police Force, called a meeting of his prohibition agents."Put both hands on the table," he snapped, and then "Every one of you sons-o-bitches with a diamond is fired." A half left.

The Rise of Al Capone

When prohibition was introduced in the U.S., a dozen large gangs were operating in Chicago in more or less clearly demarcated territories. Al Capone's boss, Johnny Torrio, was the owner of one such territory.

The Outfit (also known as the Chicago Outfit, the Chicago Mafia, the Chicago Mob, the Chicago crime family, the South Side Gang or The Organization) was one such gang -- an Italian-American organized crime syndicate based in Chicago, Illinois, dating back to the 1910s. The Outfit rose to power in the 1920s under the control of Johnny Torrio and the Prohibition era was marked by bloody gang wars for control of the distribution of illegal alcohol. The O'Donnell gang started hijacking beer trucks belonging to Johnny Torrio and this called for retaliation. Torrio summoned Al

Capone, then 21, from New York City to Chicago. Torrio actually did not like violence. He believed more in reconciliation, while Al Capone was the reverse. Within two years, using the time tested twin methods of bribery and violence, Al Capone became very powerful. He had the audacity to kill openly in public without any fear, because no one dared to testify against him. Torrio had full faith in Al Capone and practically made Al Capone his partner.

It was easy to obtain acquittals in Chicago during the Prohibition era. Al Capone made news by shaking hands with Joe Howard, a bootlegger, in a crowded bar on 8 May 1924 and then pumping six bullets into his body. Next day, the newspapers carried Al Capone's photograph and the news that he had murdered Joe Howard by firing six bullets from a revolver in a crowded bar. But with no further evidence, the inquest jury had to conclude that Howard was murdered with bullets fired from a revolver by unknown white persons.

Al Capone and his mentor Johnny Torrio started earning at least one million dollar a week. In October 1924, a dispute arose between the Gennas and O'Banion gangs. Al Capone and Torrio seized this opportunity and killed Dion O'Banion on 10 November 1924 at his flower shop. O'Banion's empire was taken over by Hymie Weiss. Hymie ordered a machine gun attack on Al Capone's car. Al Capone was ambushed on 12 January 1925 leaving him shaken, but unhurt. Twelve days later, on 24 January 1925, Torrio was returning from a shopping trip with his wife Anna. He was shot several times. Torrio recovered, but he effectively resigned and handed over control of the Outfit to Al Capone. Al Capone became the new boss of the Outfit at the age of 26.

On 20 September 1926, at 1.15 P.M., Al Capone had just finished lunch at the ground level restaurant in Hawthorne Inn. A black car raced down the street. It looked like a detective car chasing escaping mobsters. A person on the running board was firing (blanks – as it was later found) from a Thomson sub- machine gun.

All the sixty customers in the restaurant (including Al Capone) rushed to the window to see the fun. A convoy of ten cars, at intervals of ten yards each, suddenly arrived and halted outside

Hawthorne Inn. Machine gun toting gunmen got down from the cars.

Al Capone's bodyguard threw him under a table. The machine gunners fired more than a thousand rounds. The restaurant was shred to pieces. But no one was killed. Al Capone re-imbursed the Hawthorne shop keepers the losses they had suffered. He also spent $ 5,000 to save the eye sight of an innocent passerby who was injured in the crossfire. Hymie was gunned down on 11 October 1926. Al Capone took over the vast criminal empire. He was extremely ruthless and systematically eradicated his opponents. Many fled. Al Capone, then only 26, became the most powerful crime lord of the day and could boast that he owned Chicago. He had over a thousand persons working under him with a weekly payroll of $ 3,00,000. On 26 October 1926, Al Capone called all the Chicago gang leaders to the Hotel Sherman for a mobster summit. This was the first mobsters' summit in the history of crime. A mutual truce was agreed upon. Chicago and Cook County were divided amongst the four main gangs. There would be no further killings! As a result of this truce, everyone made money. But Al Capone became extremely wealthy. He ran his empire from Salone 430 – a six room suite on the fourth floor of Hotel Sherman. But eventually occupancy declined. Hotel Sherman closed its doors in early 1973. The building stood vacant for several years, until it was torn down in 1980 to make way for a new State of Illinois office center.

The bootleggers of Chicago had direct connections with the Mayor. Al Capone is believed to have played a direct role in bringing about the victories of Republican William Hale Thompson who was mayor during 1915 to 1923. Thomson again contested the 1927 mayoral race. He campaigned for a wide-open town, at one time hinting that he would reopen illegal saloons. Al Capone supported Thompson and he allegedly contributed of $ 2,50,000. Thompson beat William Emmett Dever by a relatively slim margin.

These elections were accompanied by high levels of violence and graft. Another politician, Joe Esposito, who became a political rival of Al Capone, was killed on 21 March 1928, in a drive-by shooting in front of his house. Al Capone continued to back Thompson. On 10 April 1928, the polling day of the so-called Pineapple Primary Voting,

Al Capone's bomber James Belcastro targeted booths in the wards where Thompson's opponents were thought to have support, causing the deaths of at least 15 people. Thompson left office on 9 April 1931. Historians rank Thompson among the most unethical and corrupt mayors in the history of U.S., mainly because of his open alliance with Al Capone.

In spite of this, Thompson was a popular mayor. But his popularity collapsed after his death, when two safe-deposit boxes were found in his name containing over $ 1.8 million ($ 27.1 million today) in cash. When the money was uncovered, the Internal Revenue Service took their share of taxes, and his wife Maysie Thompson lived off the remaining money until her death in 1958.

Al Capone's net annual income during his heydays has been estimated at $ 125 million. Al Capone was a conservative family man. He dressed immaculately in custom made silk shirts. He donated generously to charities and contributed lavishly for deserving causes. He loved to attend press conferences and premier shows of operas and distributed tips in hundred dollar notes.

St. Valentine's Day Massacre

In early 1929, Bugs Moran started stealing consignments belonging to Al Capone and threatening his men. Al Capone ordered his elimination. On St. Valentine's Day, 14 October 1929, Al Capone's men, dressed as police officers, shot dead a number of Moran's aides. But Moran was lucky. Because of some delay, he had not arrived at the place and survived. No one was ever charged for these murders. But Al Capone had effectively finished Moran's criminal career.

U.S. President names Al Capone Public Enemy No. 1

Al Capone enjoyed a Robin Hood type of image in the public. But the St. Valentine's Day Massacre drew a lot of public criticism. The American public had had enough of Al Capone. The St. Valentine's Day massacre was the last straw. In the wake of the Saint Valentine's Day Massacre, Walter A. Strong, publisher of the Chicago Daily News, decided to request his friend President Herbert Clark Hoover for federal intervention to stem Chicago's lawlessness.

On 19 March 1929, just two weeks after Hoover had become President, Strong arranged a secret meeting at the White House. Frank Loesch of the Chicago Crime Commission, and Laird Bell, a distinguished lawyer were also present in the meeting. They presented their case to the President. In his 1952 Memoir, President Hoover has written that Strong argued: "Chicago was in the hands of the gangsters, that the police and magistrates were completely under their control ...that the Federal Government was the only force by which the city's ability to govern itself could be restored. At once I directed that all the Federal agencies concentrate upon Mr. Capone and his allies."

President Herbert Hoover named Al Capone Public Enemy No. 1 and ordered action against him. Various wings of the American Government – the Prohibition Bureau, Federal Bureau of Investigation, Justice Department, Treasury Department and others, discussed ways and means to put away Al Capone.

The Justice Department smashed up his breweries and seized his trucks. But these losses hardly had any impact on Al Capone's empire. He was simply too big to be bothered by these petty losses. The Treasury Department put agent Frank J. Wilson, a senior investigator of the Special Intelligence Unit, after him.

Al Capone claimed he was earning less than $ 5,000 a year, the threshold limit for paying income tax in the U.S., and therefore his income was not taxable. As a result, he was not required to file any returns of income or pay any income tax. Al Capone did not have any property in his name. He did not even have a bank account in his name. All his assets were in the name of benamidars.

It was difficult, if not impossible, to collect details of Al Capone's income. Systematically and laboriously, Frank Wilson collected details of Al Capone's expenses. Between 1926 and 1929, his expenditure was $ 1,65,000. He had purchased furniture worth $ 25,000, spent $ 7,000 on suits and paid $ 40,000 for telephone calls. These evidences were sufficient to secure a conviction - but for a maximum period of three years. Wilson persuaded Al Capone's casino employees to give evidence against him. Ultimately, on 5 June 1931, Al Capone was indicted for failure to pay taxes on one million dollars of undisclosed income. The maximum possible term of imprisonment now was thirty years.

Al Capone's attorneys agreed to plead guilty on condition that he would get not more than two years imprisonment. But the Judge came to know about this unholy agreement and he refused to accept it. So Al Capone was tried. And in spite of persistent threats on the jurors and bribery offers resulting in last minute change of the entire jury, Al Capone was found guilty on all counts.

Al Capone Jailed for Tax Evasion

On 17 October 1931, Al Capone, Public Enemy No. 1, was indicted. A week later, he was sentenced to 11 years imprisonment and fine of $ 50,000 plus $ 7,692 for court costs. He was also held liable for $ 215,000 plus interest due on his back taxes – the most severe sentence imposed for a tax offence till that time. His appeals were dismissed.

Al Capone, aged 33, was sent to Atlanta U.S. Penitentiary in May 1932. Upon his arrival at Atlanta, Al Capone was officially diagnosed with syphilis and gonorrhea. He was also suffering from withdrawal symptoms from cocaine addiction, the use of which had perforated his nasal septum. In prison, he was seen as a weak personality, and fellow inmates bullied him. His cellmate, seasoned convict Red Rudensky, feared that Al Capone would have a breakdown and he became a protector for Al Capone.

In August 1934, Al Capone was moved to the recently opened Alcatraz Federal Penitentiary or United States Penitentiary on Alcatraz Island, 1.25 miles (2.01 km) off the coast of San Francisco, California, U.S.

America's honeymoon with prohibition had been a complete disaster. Prohibition was repealed by the Twenty First Amendment in 1933. And the despised alcohol became the Westerner's drink of choice. To complete the story, while in prison Al Capone was diagnosed to be suffering from Syphilis. He was released on parole on 19 November 1939 after spending 6 ½ years in prison. By this time, the disease had reached the tertiary stage and he was approaching madness. He lived for another seven years with his wife in Florida.

His end came on 25 January 1947. He died due to brain haemorrhage and was buried in grand style in a marble mausoleum at Mt. Olive in Chicago.

Al Capone gave the public what they wanted – drugs, gambling and prostitution and earned their support. Though he is reputed to have ordered the murder of at least 500 persons and an equal number died in the inter-rival gang wars, he set a trend which successive gang leaders tried to emulate.

Al Capone's conviction showed that it may be very difficult to produce direct evidence of criminal activity, it is far easier to prosecute cases for tax evasion. Al Capone's conviction made even criminals realize that it was not enough to earn illegal money, they must also launder the money. In fact, his conviction and imprisonment laid the foundation stone of the present day art and practice of money laundering.

What happened to Capone's wealth?

Some people believe that Capone had left behind a lot of money – probably hidden somewhere. And this is what the gossips and stories say. After all, he had earned so much. The entire money could not just vanished! But where had he hidden the money?

Marie Capone, Capone's niece, wrote that her uncle had buried and hidden millions of dollars in notes. But when he was released from prison, he was mentally too ill, and could not remember where he had hidden the money.

Various guesses and conjectures were made and searches conducted. But the money has not been found.

In the early 1980s, a local women's construction company called Sunbow examined the possibility of restoring the Lexington Hotel, which by then was far different from the luxurious place that Al Capone had patronized. As the work crew surveyed the building, they discovered a secret shooting range that had been used by Al Capone's men for target practice and dozens of hidden tunnels that connected to nearby bars and brothels and were designed to provide elaborate escape routes from police raids and attacks by rivals.

This led to more interest in the hotel and attracted researcher Harold Rubin to the crumbling old building. Rubin began a meticulate search of the premises. In addition to recovering many priceless artifacts from the days of the hotel's glory, Rubin stumbled across what seemed to be secret vaults where Al Capone had stashed some of his money. The vaults which had been a mere rumor for years were so expertly hidden that even Al Capone's closest accomplices were not aware of them.

Rubin's discovery was reported in the Chicago Tribune. But his research was soon overshadowed by the arrival of Geraldo Rivera, American investigative journalist, who announced that if the secret money vaults were going to be opened, he would do it and he would do this live on national television.

In April 1986, Rivera and his camera crew came to Chicago. On 21 April 1986, they began a live broadcast titled "The Mystery of Al Capone's Vaults" from the abandoned hotel.

The show aired on ABC was sensationally marketed and seen by millions of viewers, who expected to see a vault stuffed with cash from the 1920s.

The crew blasted away a 7,000-pound concrete wall in a basement chamber, which was believed to be hiding a secret compartment that contained millions of dollars.

IRS agents waited nearby, ready to seize their share of the cash. But when the smoke cleared, the vault was found to contain nothing more than a few empty bottles and an old sign. If there had ever been any money there, it had vanished long ago.

The TV show had a disastrous flop ending, but remains the most-watched TV special in history, with an audience of over 30 million.

The Lexington Hotel finally "gave up the ghost" in November 1995. By that time, after years of neglect, the 10-story structure had fallen into complete ruins and it was torn down. Another chapter in the history of Chicago crime had been shut for ever.

Al Capone's wealth has been estimated at 100 million U.S dollars. What about the money? What happened to it? Well, it is still missing.

If it ever existed at all – and wasn't spent years ago, it is lying hidden somewhere, waiting for some lucky person to find it!

Al Capone bought a fabulous mansion in Miami, Florida in 1928, at the age of 29. This house, now renamed *93 Palm Island*, was built in 1922. He bought the house in his wife's name for $ 40,000 and reportedly spent $ 200,000 to install the gatehouse, seven-foot-high wall, searchlights, a cabana and coral rock grotto. Al Capone died in his bedroom in this house on 25 January 1947, at the age of 48. The house remained in his family until 1952 when it was sold by his wife, Mae Capone.

The house has a private beach, lovely gardens and is the best property in Miami. This mansion has been purchased in July 2020 by an unnamed party for $ 10.85 million.

Capone's Family

Al Capone married Mary Josephine Coughlin at the St. Mary Star of the Sea Church in Brooklyn, New York on 30 December 1918. Her parents had immigrated to the U.S. from Ireland separately in the 1890s. Mary was known as Mae. She was two years older than her husband. On their marriage certificate, Al Capone increased his own age by one year, and decreased Mae's age by two years, making them both appear 20 years old.

They had a son Albert Francis "Sonny" Capone. From a young age, Sonny showed signs of being hard of hearing. This was probably because of the syphilis he had inherited from his parents. When Sonny developed a mastoid ear infection, doctors in Chicago said that treating the infection would leave Sonny permanently deaf. Al Capone and Mae travelled from Chicago to New York to get him the best medical treatment. Al Capone reached out to a doctor in New York City and offered $100,000 to treat his son. The doctor charged the customary $1,000. He managed to salvage Sonny's hearing, although the boy became partially deaf. Sonny attended the prestigious St. Patrick School in Miami Beach, Florida, where he befriended the young Desiderio Arnaz - known to the world today, as Desi Arnaz,

Desi Arnaz and his wife Lucille Ball jointly founded the Desilu Productions, an American Television production company. This company is famous for super hit television shows such as I Love Lucy, The Lucy Show, Mannix, The Untouchables, Mission: Impossible and Star Trek.

Sonny went to college at Notre Dame but finished his studies at the University of Miami. Sonny could have become a Don like his father, but his mother persuaded Sonny to follow the straight and more difficult path. When Al Capone died, Sonny was at his father's side.

Following the release of the TV series, *The Untouchables*, Mae filed a lawsuit when her grandchildren were being bullied in school for being a Capone.

In 1966, Sonny changed his name to Albert Francis Brown and lived under the new identity. According to his lawyer, Sonny Capone did so because he was "just sick and tired of fighting the name." After changing his name, Albert Francis Capone, aka Sonny Capone, aka Albert Francis Brown lived a quiet, law-abiding life. After his father's death, Sonny continued to live in Florida and worked as an apprentice printer, then as a tyre distributor, and later as a restaurant owner.

Sonny married three times and is survived by numerous children, grand children, and great grand children. He died on 8 July 2004 in the tiny California town of Auburn Lake Trails. His wife, America "Amie" Francis, told a reporter that Albert Francis Capone was much more than his family name.

Mae was not involved in Al Capone's racketeering business, although she was hurt by the actions Al Capone took in dating other women while they were married. She once told her son "not to do what your father did. He broke my heart." Her hair also started to grey when she was 28, presumably due to stress regarding her husband's situation.

After Al Capone was sentenced to 11 years imprisonment on 24 October 1931, Mae was one of three persons allowed to visit him in prison. The other two persons allowed to visit Al Capone in prison were his mother and their son Sonny. Mae remained a devoted wife, frequently writing letters to her husband, referring to him as "honey", and longing for him to return home. She visited him in the prison as well, travelling up to 3,000 miles from their Florida home to Alcatraz, usually taking great care to hide her face in order to avoid the paparazzi. From Al Capone's imprisonment until his death, Mae, along with Capone's brothers and sisters, was in charge of his affairs: possessions, titles, and belongings.

Al Capone was finally released from prison and arrived at their Florida home on 22 March 1940. After his release from prison, Mae was his primary caretaker. He died on 25 January 1947, in their Miami home and was buried in a Catholic Cemetery in Hillside, Illinois. Mae was distraught by his death, and remained out of the public spotlight thereafter.

Al Capone's racketeering business earned him a lot of money. Sometime between the years 1920-1921, he bought a home in Chicago that housed Mae and Sonny, as well as members of the Capone family. Mae and Sonny did not move from Brooklyn to Chicago to join Al Capone until 1923. He also bought a second home for his family in Palm Isle, Florida. Mae decorated this home lavishly.
The family owned several cars - a couple of Lincolns and a custom designed Cabriolet (similar to a Cadillac) which Mae drove herself. They lived comfortably, and had enough money to live luxuriously. They were once even burglarized at their Palm Island home. An estimated $ 300,000 worth of Mae's jewellery was stolen.

In 1936, the federal government raised a tax lien of $ 51,498.08 on Capone's Miami estate. This estate had been purchased in Mae's name. Since Al Capone was in jail, Mae was left to deal with the lien. She paid it. In 1937, she filed a lawsuit against J. Edwin Larsen, the Collector for the Internal Revenue Service, claiming that the tax lien money had been collected illegally. Her request for a refund of $ 52,103.30 was denied.

In 1959, Desilu Productions, Inc. released a two-part series called *The Untouchables*. The series was about Prohibition Agents fighting crime. In 1960, Mae, her son, and Al Capone's sister, Mafalda Maritote, sued Desilu Productions, Inc., Columbia Broadcasting

System and Westinghouse Electric Corporation, for $ 6 million in damages. They claimed the series infringed on their privacy and had caused them humiliation and shame. Sonny claimed that his children had been made fun of in school, so much that he was forced to pack up and move his family to another city. The Federal District Court and Chicago Circuit Court rejected the suit. The Capones appealed to the U.S. Supreme Court. But their appeal was rejected on the ground that privacy rights are personal and do not extend to the next of kin.

Mae died on 16 April 1986 at the age of 89, in a nursing home in Hollywood, Florida. She was buried in Florida.

After Al Capone

The immediate impact of Al Capone's conviction was that on his imprisonment, he ceased to be boss. The government officials involved in jailing Al Capone portrayed this as if they had smashed the city's organized crime syndicate.

Paul De Lucia, known as Paul Ricca, an Italian-American mobster became the nominal or de facto leader of the Chicago Outfit. He remained there for 40 years. He was the brain behind the operations of Al Capone and his successors.

Francesco Raffaele Nitto or Frank Nitti was born on 27 January 1886, in the small town of Angri, province of Salerno, Campania, Italy. He and his mother migrated to the U.S. in June 1893. He was a first cousin of Al Capone. He moved to Chicago around 1913, worked as a barber where he made the acquaintance of gangsters Alex Louis Greenberg and Dion O'Banion.

Nitti came to the notice of Torrio. But it was under Torrio's successor Al Capone, that Nitti's reputation soared. Nitti ran Al Capone's liquor smuggling and distribution operations, importing whisky from Canada and selling it through a network of speakeasies around Chicago. Nitti became one of Al Capone's top lieutenants, trusted for his leadership skills and business acumen. Because Nitti's ancestry was from the same town as Al Capone, Nitti was able to help Al Capone penetrate the Sicilian and Camorra underworld in a way Al Capone alone never could.

On 17 May 1929, Al Capone and his bodyguard were arrested in Philadelphia for carrying concealed deadly weapons. Within 16 hours, they were sentenced to terms of one year each. Al Capone served his time and was released on 17 March 1930 - in ten months for good behavior.

Al Capone thought very highly of Nitti and when he went to prison in 1929, he named Nitti as a member of a triumvirate that would run the Outfit in his absence. Nitti was head of operations. Jake "Greasy Thumb" Guzik was head of administration and Tony "Joe Batters" Accardo was made head of enforcement. Nitti was also known as "The Enforcer". And this is what he used to do in the early days. But as he rose up the ranks, he used Mafia soldiers and others to commit violence rather than do it himself.

In 1931, both Al Capone and his underboss Frank Nitti were convicted of tax evasion and sent to prison. However, Nitti received an 18-month sentence which he served at the United States Penitentiary, Leavenworth; while Al Capone was sent away for 11 years.

When Nitti was released on 25 March 1932, he took his place as the new boss of the Outfit. Far from being smashed, the Outfit continued without being troubled by the Chicago police, at a lower level and without the open violence that had marked Al Capone's rule. Once prohibition was repealed, organized crime in the city had a lower profile. The gangsters worked more secretively. Prostitution, labour union racketeering and gambling became money makers for organized crime in the city without inviting serious investigation. In the late 1950s, FBI agents discovered an organization led by Capone's former lieutenants reigning supreme over the Chicago underworld.

Womens' stand on the 18th Amendment – Prohibition

There was controversy among women in the U.S. concerning the 18th Amendment. Organizations such as the Woman's Christian Temperance Union (WCTU) supported the 18th Amendment and fought to uphold it. This organization was viewed as being representative of all women and many assumed that women would stand united on this subject. However, this notion fell apart with the rise of the Women's Organization for National Prohibition Reform (WONPR).

Both groups were centered around the protection of the home, but had radically different opinions on how this could be accomplished. While the WCTU believed that the home needed to be protected from the influences of alcohol, the WONPR protested against the cultural effects of prohibition. They saw the Amendment as the cause of the increased crime and an attitude of resentment for the law.

Many believed that the 19th Amendment allowing women to vote would be the sustaining power behind the 18th Amendment, but women were a highly influential force in overturning it. During all this political unrest, Mae remained silent. Despite being married to one of the biggest names in bootlegging, she never voiced any opinion on prohibition. She certainly benefited from the Amendment, as it created the demand for her husband's line of work and made them richer, but she never expressed her views about the matter in public. It is believed that she actively discouraged her son Sonny from following his father's footsteps.

During this era, many women took the opportunity to step out of anonymity and hog the public limelight. But Mae sought anonymity and avoided the press. Even when wives of other gangsters were coming out and writing books about their experiences regarding being married to mob leaders, Mae did not write or publish anything for the public. While other women fought to end prohibition, she fought for privacy. Sonny died on 8 July 2004 at the age of 85.

In the early 1940s, a handful of top Outfit leaders went to prison because they were found to be extorting money from Hollywood by controlling the unions that compose Hollywood's movie industry, and manipulating and misusing the Teamsters Central States Pension fund. In 1943, the Outfit was caught red-handed shaking down the Hollywood movie industry. Ricca wanted Nitti to take the blame. However, years earlier while in jail for 18 months (for tax evasion) Nitti had found that he was claustrophobic. And he decided to end his life rather than face more imprisonment for extorting Hollywood. Ricca then became the boss in name, as well as in fact, with enforcement chief Tony Accardo as underboss - the start of a partnership that lasted for almost 30 years.

From 1997 to 2018, the Chicago Outfit is believed to have been led by John DiFronzo. As of 2022, the Chicago Outfit is believed to be led by the 83 year old Salvatore "Solly D" DeLaurentis.

The Golden Triangle

The two principal regions for supply of opiates throughout the world are the 'Golden Triangle' and the 'Golden Crescent'.

Since the 1950s, Golden Triangle and the Golden Crescent have been the two largest opium-producing areas of the world. Until the early 21st century, most of the world's heroin came from the Golden Triangle. After that, the Golden Crescent has become the world's largest producer. From 1998 to 2006, following an eradication campaign in the area, poppy cultivation in the Golden Triangle decreased more than 80 percent. But synthetic drug production has expanded. The Golden Triangle is now one of the world's leading areas for the production and supply of synthetic drugs - particularly methamphetamine.

Khun Sa - King of the Golden Triangle

The Golden Triangle comprises of some 950,000 square kilometers (367,000 square miles) of impassable mountainous jungles situated on the intersection of Myanmar, Laos and Thailand. This area is bounded by the Mekong and Mae si Rivers. Native people called Shan inhabit this area.

When the Chinese Civil War ended with the defeat of the Chinese National Army in 1949, thousands of the defeated Kuomintang troops crossed over the border from Yunnan province into Myanmar (then Burma) and entered this impassable terrain. U.S. supplied them arms and money for over a decade.

In the late 1950s, the Myanmar Government went after these people and pushed them towards Thailand and Laos. U.S. stopped overt help, but the CIA continued to use Khun Sa to collect information about the communists and therefore supported them for the next two decades. Pursued by the Myanmar Government; and with the major portion of their supplies stopped, the Nationalists entered the business of cultivation of opium poppy, which had been the staple cash crop in the area.

Khun Sa was born on 17 February 1934. His original name was Chang Chi Fu. After 40 years, he changed his name Chang Chi Fu to Khun Sa - the Burmese Shan dialect for "Prince Prosperous". He renamed his group the Shan United Army and began to claim that he was fighting against the Burmese government for the autonomy of Shan. Khun Sa was one of the most powerful and notorious Burmese warlords and drug lord. He was known as "the Prince of Death" and "King of the Golden Triangle".

Khun Sa started manufacturing and exporting heroin to the U.S. Apart from manufacturing heroin for smoking, he also manufactured heroin suitable for intravenous injection. This new, pure, heroin could be snorted or smoked, cutting the link between intravenous injection and HIV infection. Gradually, he expanded his operations and started shipping heroin to Bangkok from where it went to various countries. Khun Sa became one of the biggest opium producers in the world.

The profits were huge. One kilogram of opium base cost around $ 3,000. But on the streets, it fetched up to a thousand times more. In 1978, Khun Sa even had the audacity to propose to the U.S. Government that he could solve their heroin problem by exporting 500 tons of opium base at a price of $ 50 million.

In 1980, the Americans were so desperate that they put a price of $ 25,000 on Khun Sa's head and requested the Thai authorities to take urgent action against him. In July 1981, Thai authorities announced a 50,000 baht ($ 2,000 U.S.) bounty on his head. In August, this was raised to 500,000 baht ($ 20,000 U.S.), "valid until 30 Sept. 1982". In October 1981, at the insistence of the U.S. Drug Enforcement Administration, a 39-man unit of Thai Rangers and local rebel guerillas attempted to assassinate Khun Sa. The attempt failed, and almost the entire unit was wiped out.

In 1982, the Thais launched a massive assault on Khun Sa's fortress in Ban Hin Tack, a small place in Chiang Rai, Thailand. Two thousand troops supported with helicopter forces killed 200 people and seized tons of equipment. But Khun Sa escaped. He returned back after two years and became only more active than before. Since the mid 1980s, the Golden Triangle overtook Mexico and Turkey, the traditional suppliers of heroin; and became the World's No. 1 supplier. During the 1980s, under Khun Sa's leadership, Burma's opium production soared from 550 to 2,500 tons – increase of an unbelievable 500 percent. Fuelled by Burma's rising poppy harvest between 1984 and 1990, Southeast Asia's share of the New York City heroin market jumped from 5 to 80 percent. By 1990, Khun Sa controlled over 80 percent of Burma's opium production -- making him history's most powerful drug lord.

This flood of Burmese heroin reduced the prices and increased the purity in the U.S. drug market. Between the mid-1980s and mid-1990s, the annual U.S. heroin supply rose from five to 10 –15 metric tons, sustaining an expanded population of 600,000 hard-core American addicts. As Burmese heroin, known on the street as "China White" landed in unprecedented quantities, the retail price in New York City dropped from $ 1.81 per milligram in 1988 to just $ 0.37 in 1994. Simultaneously, the national average for heroin content of "street deals" rose from just 7 to 40 percent, reaching 63 percent in New York City and even higher elsewhere. On the streets, unknown entrepreneurs – negotiating the variables of price, purity, supply, and market – dealt with this surge in supply by raising purity and changing the drug's demographics.

In 1985, Khun Sa merged his Shan United Army with another rebel group, the "Tai Revolutionary Council" of Moh Heng, a faction of the Shan United Revolutionary Army (SURA), forming the Mong Tai Army (MTA). Through this strategic alliance, he gained control of a 150-mile Thai-Burma border area from his base at Ho Mong, a village near Mae Hong Son, to Mae Sai.

In December 1989, a U.S. grand jury indicted Khun Sa in absentia for trying to smuggle 1,500 kilograms of heroin into the U.S. between 1986 and 1988. So long he was in his home country, all this made little difference to Khun Sa. His only worry was the fear of abduction, followed by trial in the U.S. as had happened in the case of the Latin American drug traffickers.

In the early 1990s, American popular culture made this cheaper, "safe" heroin the signifier of an alienated authenticity. Cult figures like Curt Cobain and River Phoenix became celebrity heroin addicts of a young decade. In May 1996, Rolling Stone magazine ran a feature on the problem titled "Rock & Roll Heroin" listing dozens of megastars with major habits.

Khun Sa headed the Shan United Army (also known as Mong Tai Army or MTA) consisting of 20,000 heads. He claimed to be taxing the opium poppy growers for financing the Shan people's fight for independence. In 1993, Khun Sa declared independence for his northern Shan State.

Khun Sa and his aides, mostly close relatives, ran their empire from the village of Wan Ho Mong which is about nine kilometers from the Thai border. 1994 was particularly bad for Khun Sa. There was severe draught. And in an effort to gain international goodwill, the Myanmar Army mounted a sustained offensive against Khun Sa. They destroyed his laboratories and tightened the border making it increasingly difficult for him to smuggle the drugs out of Myanmar. The Myanmar Army continued the offensive against Khun Sa during 1995. On 22 November 1995, Khun Sa announced that he had relinquished command of the Shan United Army. On 2 January 1996, the Myanmar troops took control of Wan Ho Mong, the headquarters of the Shan United Army. Khun Sa surrendered to the Myanmar military junta. Political observers speculated that the peaceful entry of military forces into Wan Ho Mong and the bloodless surrender of Khun Sa suggested that all this was due to some pre-negotiated arrangement and that the Myanmar army had offered Khun Sa amnesty and a guarantee against extradition. By 28 January 1996, 11,739 members of the Shan United Army had surrendered.

On 4 January 1996, the U.S. Government offered reward of U.S. $ 2,00,000 for information leading to the arrest and conviction of Khun Sa. The political observers were proved right when on 9 February 1996, U. Ohn Gyaw, the Myanmar Foreign Minister formally announced that his Government would not extradite Khun Sa to the U.S. However, Khun Sa's surrender was not expected to reduce the export of opium. Drug traffickers like Chao Nyi Lai and others simply moved into the void created by him.

On 5 January 1996, Khun Sa gave up control of his army and moved to Rangoon with a large fortune and four young Shan mistresses. Following Khun Sa's surrender, opium production in the Golden Triangle declined and opium production in the Golden Crescent rose dramatically. After his retirement, Khun Sa became a prominent local businessman, with investments in Yangon, Mandalay and Taunggyi. He described himself as "a commercial real estate agent with a foot in the construction industry". He ran a large ruby mine, and invested in a new highway running from Yangon to Mandalay. While living in Yangoon, Khun Sa maintained a low profile. His movements and communications with the outside world were restricted by the Burmese government, and his activities were monitored by Burmese intelligence.

On 31 May 1999, Khun Sa was reported to have been paralyzed for some months. He also regretted his decision to surrender to the Burmese authorities in December 1995. Khun Sa died on 26 October 2007 in Yangon at the age of 73. Though he had suffered from diabetes, high blood pressure, and heart disease, the cause of his death is not known, He was cremated four days after his death. His remains were buried at Yayway Cemetery, North Okkalapa, Yangon, Myanmar.

Soon after Khun Sa's death, a memorial was held for him in November 2007, in his former stronghold in Thailand, Thoed Thai, close to the Myanmar border. When the local people were asked why they honoured Khun Sa, they said that he had helped develop the town. He built the first paved roads in the area; the first school; and a well-equipped, 60 bed hospital staffed by Chinese doctors. He was building a hydro power plant, but after his departure, construction on that project was halted. He also built an 18-hole golf course for foreign visitors and a functional water and electrical infrastructure. The local Thai authorities ensured that the ceremony remained relatively simple and low profile.

Khun Sa was married to Nan Kyayon (died 1993) with whom he had eight children - five sons and three daughters. All of Khun Sa's children were educated abroad. As a reward for his retirement and relocation to Yangon, the Government allowed his children to run and operate business interests in Myanmar. At the time of his death, his favorite son was running a hotel and casino in the border town of Tachilek, while one of his daughters was a well-established business woman in Mandalay. All his children are occupied in respectable businesses.

Shan State represents the main opium producing region in Myanmar, accounting for 82% (331 metric tons) of the country's total output (405 metric tons) in 2020. Since 2015, opium poppy cultivation has declined year after year. In 2020, cultivation in Shan State declined a further 12%, with reductions taking place in East, North and South Shan with respective decreases of 17%, 10% and 9% from previous levels in 2019.

Under the 2010 Constitution of Myanmar, Shan State (commonly known by its native name Muang Tai) is now a state of the Republic of the Union of Myanmar (Burma), with its own Government. The first General elections were held in November 2010 and the first Government was formed in 2011. The area occupied by the Shan State is 155,801.3 sq. kms (60,155.2 sq. miles). The population is 5,824,432 (2014).

Wa State and Chao Nyi Lai

The Wa State is the name given to the Wa Land, the natural and historical region inhabited mainly by the Wa tribal people. The area north and east of Khun Sa's territory is inhabited by the Wa tribe. Wa State is divided into northern and southern regions which are separated from each other.

On 17 April 1989, ethnic Wa soldiers split from the Communist Party of Burma and established the United Wa State Army (UWSA) consisting of an estimated 20,000 – 25,000 Wa soldiers led by Bao Youxiang and ended the long-running Communist insurgency in Burma. On 9 May 1989, the Burmese government signed a cease-fire agreement with UWSA, formally ending the conflict. The cease-fire agreement allowed the United Wa State Army to freely expand their logistical operations with the Burmese military, including the trafficking of drugs to neighbouring Thailand and Laos.

The United Wa State Army was founded and led by Chao Ngi Lai (1939–2009) and later by Bao Youxiang. It is strongly supported by China, which gives more support to it than to the Myanmar government.

The Wa people have also nurtured hopes for independence. But unlike the Shans, their relations with Myanmar were quite cordial. In fact, the relations of all the drug barons, except Khun Sa, with the military have always been quite cordial. It used to be quite common to see the drug traffickers playing golf with the Myanmar military generals in Yangon.

The United Wa State Army (UWSA) was previously the largest narcotics trafficking organization in Southeast Asia. The UWSA cultivated opium poppy over vast areas of land, which was later refined to heroin. Methamphetamine trafficking was also important to the economy of Wa State. The money from the opium was primarily used for purchasing weapons.

In August 1990, government officials began drafting a plan to end drug production and trafficking in Wa State. Bao Youxiang and Zhao Nyi-Lai went to Cangyuan Va Autonomous County of China and signed the Cangyuan Agreement with local officials, which stated that, "No drugs will go into the international society (from Wa State); no drugs will go into China (from Wa State); no drugs will go into Burmese government-controlled areas (from Wa State)." However, the agreement did not mention whether or not Wa State could sell drugs to insurgent groups.

Until 1996, the United Wa State Army was involved in conflict against the Shan Mong Tai Army led by the drug lord Khun Sa. During this conflict, the Wa State Army occupied areas close to the Thai border, ending up with the control of two separate swathes of territory north and south of Kengtung. In 1997, the United Wa State Party officially proclaimed that Wa State would be drug-free by the end of 2005. With the help of the United Nations and the Chinese government, many opium farmers in Wa State shifted to production of rubber and tea. However, some poppy farmers continued to cultivate opium poppy outside of Wa State.

The Burmese government started taking measures to decrease the production of such drugs. But this was an arduous task due to corruption at high levels in the government and a lack of infrastructure to carry out operations. In 2005, the UWSP declared Wa State a "drug-free zone" and the cultivation of opium was made illegal.

Opium cultivations spreads

Following an eradication campaign in the Golden Triangle, from 1998 to 2006, poppy cultivation in the area decreased more than 80 percent. Officials with the United Nations Office of Drugs and Crime have confirmed that since 2014, opium poppy farming had decreased but synthetic drug production had expanded. Moreover, opium cultivation had gradually spread all over the world. On 1 January 2009, UWSA announced its territory as the "Wa State Government Special Administrative Region". Bao Youxiang became the de facto President and Xiao Minliang the Vice President. Although the Government of Myanmar does not officially recognize the sovereignty of Wa State, the Tatmadaw (Myanmar Armed Forces) has frequently allied with the UWSA to fight against Shan nationalist militia groups, such as the Shan State Army - South.

Despite being de facto independent from Myanmar, the Wa State officially recognizes Myanmar's sovereignty over all its territory. In 1989, the two parties signed a ceasefire agreement, and in 2013 signed a peace deal.

Wei Hsueh-kang

Wei Hsueh-kang was the middle of three brothers. They were connected with the Kuomintang-CIA spy network along the Yunnan frontier until the Burmese communists drove them out in the 1970s. The eldest brother has since died.

Wei Hsueh-kang subsequently joined the late drug lord Khun Sa's Mong Tai Army (MTA), and became treasurer to Khun Sa. Wei was later briefly detained by Khun Sa. After being released by Khun Sa, Wei fled to Thailand and later traveled to Taiwan. After splitting from Khun Sa, Wei and his brothers set up a heroin empire In Thailand, along the Thai border with Myanmar and made a fortune. He was also allegedly involved in killing some of Khun Sa's men in a revenge hit in northern Thailand.

In 1986, Wei was arrested and detained in Thailand. He was sentenced to death. But he escaped and never returned to the country. In Thailand, he was known as Prasit Chiwinnitipanya, but his Thai nationality was eventually revoked.

In 1989, when the Wa rebels reached a ceasefire deal with the Myanmar junta, then known as the State Law and Order Restoration Council (SLORC), Wei returned to Panghsang. He bankrolled the Wa leadership, who at that time were cash-starved and looking for assistance of several million dollars to rebuild the Wa region and their army.

Wei who was one of the founders of the UWSA became one of its most prominent politburo members. One seasoned observer described him as the Wa's "ATM machine".

Since 1993, U.S. has offered a US $ 2 million (2.7 billion kyats, at today's rate) bounty for information leading to Wei's capture or death, as a heroin trafficker.

At one time, Wei served as a commander in the UWSA and helped Myanmar troops attack the stronghold of Khun Sa, who finally surrendered to the junta in 1996. Wei was allowed to take control of that MTA area.

In any case, the truce with the regime gave the Wa and other ethnic militias operating in the area, including Kokang insurgents, the opportunity to develop one of the largest drug-running operations in Southeast Asia.

In 1998, nine years after the Wa leaders signed a truce with the SLORC, Wei founded the Hong Pang Group based in Panghsang with revenues from the drug trade.

The Hong Pang Group invested in construction, agriculture, gems and minerals, petroleum, electronics and communications, distilleries and department stores. Hong Pang Group opened offices in Yangon, Mandalay, Lashio, Tachilek and Mawlamyine. Hong Pang Group served as the UWSA's commercial wing, growing into one of the biggest conglomerates in Myanmar, as also carrying on one of the biggest money-laundering operations in Southeast Asia.

In 2012, the Hong Pang Group was renamed Thawda Win Co. Ltd., and it remains involved in several large projects in Myanmar. The company's income also supports the UWSA's operations in Panghsang. One of the projects recently undertaken by the company is the Taung Gyi-Meikktila-Tachilek Highway. Other businesses run by Wa leaders and tycoons include banks and airlines. Wei knows that he is wanted by the U.S. and Thailand. He spends most of his time in China and along the Myanmar border. He does not allow his photos to be published.

Lao Ta Saenlee - Grandaddy of Golden Triangle drug warlords

Lao Ta Saenlee is the oldest surviving associate of Khun Sa. Surprisingly, he acquired a benevolent aura of fighting against drug abuse.

On 12 June 2003, Lao Ta, 63, believed to be a key lieutenant of Wei Hsueh-Kang, the biggest drug baron in the Golden Triangle region, and his two sons Vijan, 28, and Sukasem, 24, were arrested in Chiang Mai province, 700 km (438 miles) north of Bangkok. For the next four to five days, Lao Ta and his two sons, were flown to Chiang Rai and Chiang Mai and paraded in press conferences by government authorities and then flown back to Bangkok. The government wanted to make a big story out of the arrest.

Lao Ta faced four separate charges of illegal possession of 336 g. of heroin, trafficking in 400 kg of heroin with intent to sell to Malaysia, hiring a gunman to murder a man in Chiang Mai's Fang district and illegal possession of firearms and ammunitions.

By 2007, the courts dismissed the drug trafficking and attempted murder charges because of insufficient evidence as a result of conflicting testimony from prosecution witnesses. Lao Ta was slapped with a 18-month jail term for illegal possession of firearms.

But by this time, he had already spent four years in jail - from 2003-2007.

Lao Ta lived in Ban Huai San close to the Thailand-Myanmar border. In the books of government authorities, Lao Ta was apparently a benevolent person - part of a program to develop villages and keep people off drugs. He was twice awarded as best village headman by Chiang Mai province. "Every week I warn our youth of the dangers of drugs," he used to tell.

But in his tiny village, Lao Ta lived a very luxurious life. He attributed all this to his 200 acres of lychee and tea plantations. He had a huge and luxurious mansion. A BMW car. A new European-style mansion nearing finishing up on the hill. His residence in Fang. Houses in Chiang Mai and $ 2 million in the bank. He also owned a small supermarket and a gasoline station on the nearby main road. He also owned 23 wives, the youngest being 18 years old. "They keep me young," he used to explain. He wore a diamond-studded Rolex wrist watch. Lao Ta admitted he used to be an opium trader, with links to former drug warlord Khun Sa, but he used to insist his hands were clean today.

The police sent a plain-clothes policewoman decoy to contact Lao Ta's drug broker and order about a kilogram of crystal meth. Lao Ta delivered it at a petrol station he owned, and his wife received the agreed payment of 550,000 baht.

Police later placed a larger order for 18.8 kg and were quoted 11 million baht. The police arrested Lao Ta, his family and associates on 11 Oct 2016, during the delivery of the drug at the petrol station. The Police also seized military grade firearms and ammunition from them.

Lao Ta, 80, and four others - his wife Asama, 70; Ms Rapeekan Saimul, 60; his son Wicharn Saenlee, 43, a former kamnan of tambon Tha Ton; and Buramee Barameekuakul, 40, all from Chiang Mai - were arrested in Chiang Mai in 2016.

and charged with drug trafficking and illegal possession of firearms.

On 13 December 2017, the Criminal Court found the five accused guilty of drug trafficking and weapons charges. Lao Ta and his wife confessed. The court commuted his death penalty to life imprisonment and reduced his wife's life imprisonment to 25 years. The couple were fined 2.5 million baht each. The Appeal Court upheld the lower court's sentences. This marked the final chapter of one of the most colourful and the oldest figure of the Golden Triangle. Lao Ta was associated with the drug business for over 60 years.

Yaba - illegal amphetamines

Opium and heroin have been replaced by yaba - illegal amphetamines. Hundreds of millions of yaba tablets are being manufactured in factories in the territory controlled by Wei's United Wa State Army (UWSA). These are pouring across the Myanmar border into Thailand and beyond. The scourge is entrapping millions of users, corrupting government officials and undermining Thai society. Thai anti-drug policy has failed miserably.

In Aug 2021, Thai Parliament passed a new narcotics bill that emphasizes prevention and treatment rather than punishment for small-scale drug users, and introduced tougher measures against organized crime, which could lead to a drop in the numbers of inmates in the overcrowded Thai prisons.

The legislation, initially approved by Prime Minister Prayuth Chan-ocha's cabinet in 2019, consolidates more than 20 existing laws relating to narcotics, some unchanged since the 1970s. These range from laws and penalties relating to drug possession, smuggling and distribution, to confiscation of assets relating to drugs and organized crime.

Chatchawan Suksumjit, a senator who chaired a Thai Joint Parliamentary Committee overseeing changes to the new narcotic laws explained "The new law shifts away from the old concept that emphasises only suppression because more suppression has not resulted in drug eradication".

"Punishment will now be divided between low level, which means drug users, who will systematically receive treatment rather than prison, while high level offenders will face more severe punishment," he clarified.

According to official figures, eighty percent of more than 300,000 inmates in the Thai penitentiary system are currently detained on drug-related charges.

The Thai Justice Minister Somsak Thepsuthin earlier said the new legislation will result in reduced sentencing for almost 50,000 inmates after it becomes law.

Jeremy Douglas, Southeast Asia and Pacific representative of United Nations Office of Drugs and Crime (UNODC), described the new bill as "positive."

"It should naturally lower the prison population which is at extreme levels," Jeremy said. "This is big for both the country and region." On 9 June 2022, Thailand became the first country in Asia to legalize cannabis. It also imposes the death penalty for certain drug offences (although there has not been a single execution for a drug offence for over 10 years). The present trend is to reduce levels of imprisonment and shift towards providing a health response to drug use).

Sam Gor and Tse Chi Lop

Sam Gor, also known as "The Company", is believed to be one of the main international crime syndicates responsible for the present operations. This group is made up of members of five different triads and was headed by Tse Chi Lop, a gangster born in Guangzhou, China. Tse Chi Lop has been arrested in Amsterdam's Schiphol airport on 22 January 2021. More about him in the next chapter.

Sam Gor is believed to be controlling 40% of the Asia-Pacific methamphetamine market, while also trafficking in

heroin and ketamine. In addition to Myanmar, the syndicate is active in several countries, including Thailand, Lao PDR, New Zealand, Australia, Japan, China and Taiwan. The syndicate is earning up to $ 8 billion per year.

Experts have estimated that in 2019, drug production and trafficking in the region generated profits of at least $ 71 billion, with methamphetamine accounting for $ 61 billion, four times of what it used to be six years ago. Today, the production and trafficking of methamphetamine is the financial backbone of transnational organized crime and the ethnic armed groups that they partner with for control of autonomous territories in Myanmar, fuelling conflict and insecurity in the country, and along its borders including border with Thailand.

Tse Chi Lop Asia-Pacific's Biggest Drug Lord

What about the drug lords in the Eastern part of the globe? Is there no one to rival Pablo Escobar, Joaquin "El Chapo" Guzman and others from Colombia and Mexico? There are! But they keep a low profile and are not much known. The last successful prosecution and conviction of a top Asian drug lord Ng Sik-ho took place in May 1975.

Ng Sik-ho - Hong Kong drug lord and triad boss

Ng Sik-ho, born in 1930, was of Teochew origin. Ng earned his nickname "Crippled Ho" or "Limpy Ho" following a leg injury sustained in a street fight. The media nicknamed him Mr. Big. During the Great Chinese Famine in the 1960s, he sneaked from Mainland China into Hong Kong.

Ng was involved in the illicit business of opium and morphine from 1967. He was married to Cheng Yuet-ying who was also actively involved in the drug trade. Ng built a drug empire covering Hong Kong, Macau, Thailand, Taiwan, Singapore, Britain and America.

Ng was arrested on 2 November 1974 on charges of smuggling 20 tons of opium and morphine from Thailand and other countries into Hong Kong. In May 1975, Ng was convicted to 30 years of imprisonment, the longest sentence imposed by a Hong Kong court till that time. His wife was subsequently arrested and convicted on 23 February 1975 to 16 years imprisonment. She was also fined 1 million yuan.

Ng became a key witness in the case against Ma Sik-chun, a former associate who was facing charges of heroin and opium trafficking. Ma Sik-chun and his younger brother Ma Sik-yu had founded the Oriental Press Group, which owns Chinese-language newspaper Oriental Daily and popular news website *on.cc* in 1969. The Ma brothers who were charged with opium smuggling and bribery in Hong Kong fled to Taiwan – the elder brother in 1977 and the younger one in 1978. They could not be brought back to Hong Kong because there was no extradition treaty between Taiwan and Hong Kong. The younger brother Ma died in Taiwan in 1992. The elder brother died in Taipei Veterans General Hospital, Taiwan on 15 June 2015. The Oriental Press Group is now being run by Ma Sik-chun's son Ricky Ma Ching-fat.

In April 1991, the Governor of Hong Kong reduced Ng's sentence by four and a half years, and he was scheduled to be released at the end of the year. But in July 1991, Ng was diagnosed with terminal liver cancer. His doctors predicted that he would not live for more than 6 weeks. His sentence was then further reduced.

Ng was released on 14 August 1991 on medical grounds after serving 16 years in jail. He was moved to the Queen Mary Hospital. He died a few weeks later on 8 September 1991 at the age of 61. His wife was released from prison in 1992.

While in jail, Ng became a Buddhist and he used to say: "Wealth is decided by the heavens; Life and death by fate".

Tse Chi Lop - Asia Pacific's biggest drug lord

Tse Chi Lop, the boss of the Asia-Pacific based international crime super-syndicate, *Sam Gor*, is one of the biggest present day drug lords. Tse was born in Guangzhou, China in 1963. He migrated to Canada in 1988. In Toronto, he became part of the Big Circle Boys, a faction of the Big Circle Gang, which was originally formed during the 1960s Cultural Revolution in China by imprisoned members of Mao's Red Guard.

In the 1990s, Tse shuttled between North America, Hong Kong, Macau, Taiwan and Southeast Asia. He rose to become a mid-ranking member of a smuggling ring that sourced heroin from the Golden Triangle - the lawless opium-producing region where the borders of Myanmar, Thailand, China and Laos meet.

In 1998, Tse was arraigned on drug-trafficking charges in the Eastern District Court of New York. He was found guilty of conspiracy to import heroin into the U.S. A potential life sentence hung over his head. Tse filed a petition through his lawyer in 2000, begging for leniency. He expressed "great sorrow" for his crime. He stated that his ailing parents needed constant care. His 12-year-old son had a lung disorder. His wife was overwhelmed. He claimed that if he was freed, he would reform and open a restaurant.

His entreaties worked. Tse was sentenced to nine years in prison which were mostly spent at the federal correctional institution in Elkton, Ohio. He was released in 2006. He was supposed to return to Canada, where he was to be under supervised release for the next four years. It is not clear when Tse returned to his old haunts in Asia, but government records show that Tse and his wife Tse Chil Lop registered a company - the China Peace Investment Group Company Ltd. in Hong Kong in 2011.

After his release, Tse quickly returned to the drug business. He picked up from where he had left. He renewed connections in mainland China, Hong Kong, Macau and the Golden Triangle. He rose to power in a few short years by creating *Sam Gor*, the Cantonese term for "Brother Number Three" (also called the Company) - an alliance of 5 triads while effectively maintaining his anonymity and enjoying life in Hong Kong and Macau. *Sam Gor* is made up of five different triads: the 14K Triad, Wo Shing Wo, Sun Yee On, Big Circle Gang and Bamboo Union. The group is associated and does business with many other local crime groups such as the Yakuza in Japan, the Satudarah mc and the Comanchero Motorcycle Club and Lebanese and other gangs in Australia.

Tse developed and adopted a unique and attractive business model that proved irresistible to his customers. If any of his drug deliveries was intercepted by the police or any other authority, he offered free replacement, or return of the deposits to the buyers.

His policy of guaranteeing his drug deliveries was very good for business, but it also put him on the radar of the police and drug enforcement agencies. In 2011, officers of the Australian Federal Police (AFP) cracked a group in Melbourne importing heroin and methamphetamine (meth). The quantities were not huge – only a few dozens of kilos. So instead of arresting the Australian drug dealers,

AFP put them under surveillance, tapping their phones and observing them closely for more than a year.

This was the beginning of Operation Kungur - a secret counter-narcotics investigation. Led by the Australian Federal Police (AFP), Operation Kungur involved about 20 agencies from Asia, North America and Europe. It was the biggest international effort ever to combat Asian drug trafficking syndicates. It encompassed authorities from Myanmar, China, Thailand, Japan, U.S. and Canada. Taiwan, while not formally part of the operation, was assisting in the investigation.

To the frustration of the Melbourne drug purchasers, their illicit product kept getting intercepted. They wanted the seized drugs replaced by Sam Gor. The Sam Gor bosses in Hong Kong were irritated. Their other drug rings in Australia were collecting their narcotics and selling them without any incident. The patience of the Sam Gor leaders wore thin. In 2013, they summoned the leader of the Melbourne cell to Hong Kong for talks. There, Hong Kong police watched the Australian meet two men.

One of the two men was Tse Chi Lop. He had the center-parted hair and casual get up of a typical middle-aged Chinese family man. However, further surveillance showed Tse was a big spender with an extra keen regard for his personal security. At home or abroad, he was always protected by a guard of up to 8 Thai kick boxers at a time, who were regularly rotated as part of his security protocol. Tse flew by private jet. He once lost $ 66 million in a single night at a Macau casino.

Tse would host lavish birthday parties every year at resorts and five-star hotels, flying in his family members and entourage in private jets. On one occasion, he stayed at a resort in Thailand for a month, hosting visitors poolside in shorts and T-shirt.

As the investigation into Tse proceeded, AFP suspected that Tse was the major trafficker supplying Australia meth and heroin, with a lucrative sideline in MDMA, commonly known as ecstasy. But the huge scale of operations of the Sam Gor became apparent only in late 2016, when Cai Jeng Ze, a young Taiwanese was arrested at the Yangon airport.

On the morning of 15 November 2016, tipped off by the DEA, Yangon Airport police had been monitoring Cai Jeng Ze at the Yangon Airport. Once they lost track of him. The Yangon Airport police had no idea who Cai Jeng Ze was. Cai was heading home to Taiwan, walking through the airport with a Jimmy Choo leather bag and two mobile phones. Cai seemed nervous, picking at his blistered hands. This tic aroused suspicion. Cai was stopped and searched. Taped to each of his thighs was a small bag containing 80 grams of ketamine, a powerful tranquilizer that doubles as a party drug. "We were very fortunate to arrest him. Actually, it was an accident," the Commanding officer later said.

Cai told the Airport police that the bags on his thighs contained a "pesticide or vitamin for flowers and plants". He claimed a friend had given them to him to pass them on to his father. Cai's flight was about to leave and there was no drug test for ketamine at the airport.

Yangon Airport police were not convinced with the explanation and held him overnight. The next day, anti-narcotic officers turned up at the airport. One officer recognized Cai from the surveillance work he'd been conducting. But Cai refused to talk. Police say that videos they later found on one of his phones explained his silence. The videos showed a crying and bound man. At least three assailants were burning his feet with a blowtorch and electrocuting him with a cattle prod. The videos also showed a sign with Chinese calligraphy saying "Loyalty to the Heaven" - a triad-related sign.

According to some AFP officers, the man who was being tortured claimed to have thrown 300 kg of meth from a boat because he mistakenly believed that a fast-approaching vessel was a law enforcement boat. The torturers were testing the veracity of the victim's claims. By filming and sharing the videos, triad members were sending a message about the penalty for disloyalty.

Cai was a meticulate chronicler of the drug syndicate's activities, but had not taken any precautions about the security of the information. The phones contained a very large number of photos and videos, social media conversations, and logs of thousands of calls and text messages.

For more than two months prior to his arrest, Cai had travelled around Myanmar finalizing a huge meth deal for the syndicate. The investigators found the screenshot of a slip from an international courier company recording the delivery of two consignments of packaging, manufactured to hold loose-leaf Chinese tea, to a Yangon address. Since at least 2012, tea packets, often containing one kilo of crystal meth each, had been cropping up in drug busts across the Asia-Pacific region.

Two days after Cai's arrest, Myanmar police raided a Yangon address, where they seized 622 kilograms of ketamine. That evening, they captured 1.1 tons of crystal meth at a Yangon jetty. The interception of the drugs was a big coup. But the Myanmar police were frustrated. Nine people were arrested, but other than Cai they were all lower-level members of the syndicate, including couriers and a driver. And they could not make Cai talk.

Then came a major breakthrough. While going through the vast collection of photos and videos on Cai's phones, an AFP investigator based in Yangon noticed a familiar face from an intelligence briefing he had attended on Asian drug traffickers about a year back. He recognized the Canadian - Tse Chi Lop. The Myanmar police invited the AFP to send a team of intelligence analysts to Yangon in early 2017 to work on Cai's phones.

After the end of the Vietnam War in 1975, Australia had become a profitable drug market for Asian gangs. For over a decade, the AFP had fed all its historic files on drug cases, large and small, into a database, which had become a treasure trove of names, chemical signatures of seized drugs, phone metadata and surveillance intelligence.

The AFP analysts cross-referenced the contents of Cai's phones with their database. They discovered photos relating to three big consignments of crystal meth that were intercepted in China, Japan and New Zealand in 2016. Later, Chinese anti-narcotics officials connected photos, telephone numbers and addresses in Cai's phones to other meth busts in China.

Earlier, the counter-narcotics police of different countries had believed that the drugs were being trafficked by different crime groups. Now it became clear that all the shipments were the work of one single organization; and Cai was "one of the top members of the mega-syndicate," which had been involved in multiple "drugs cases, smuggling and manufacturing, within this region."

Cai was found not guilty in the ketamine case, but is still in jail in Yangon, where he is on trial for drug trafficking charges related to the meth seizures.

Meth Paradise

The Police suspected that during his time in Myanmar, Cai was travelling all over the country, testing drug samples, organizing couriers and obtaining a fishing boat to transport the illicit cargo to a bigger vessel in international waters. His phones contained pictures of the vehicles to be used to transport the meth, the spot where the meth was to be dropped off, and the fishing boat.

The Police's reconstruction of Cai's dealings in Myanmar led to another major revelation: The epicenter of meth production had shifted from China's southern provinces to Shan State in Myanmar's northeastern borderlands. Operations in China had provided the Sam Gor syndicate easy access to precursor ingredients, such as ephedrine and pseudoephedrine, that were smuggled out of pharmaceutical, chemical and paint factories in the Pearl River Delta Economic Zone. Shan State gave Sam Gor the freedom to operate largely unimpeded by law enforcement agencies.

Armed rebel groups in semi-autonomous regions like Shan State have long controlled large tracts of territory and used drug revenues to finance their frequent battles with the military. A series of détentes brokered by the Myanmar government with rebel groups over the years has brought relative calm to the region - and allowed illicit drug activities to flourish.

"Production facilities can be hidden from law enforcement and other prying eyes but insulated from disruptive violence," analyst Richard Horsey wrote in a paper for the International Crisis Group. "Drug production and profits are now so vast that they dwarf the formal sector of Shan State."

Travellers to the village of Loikan in Shan State can see drug-fueled prosperity. The two-lane road skirts a deep ravine known as the "Valley of Death," where ethnic Kachin rebels from the Kaung Kha paramilitary group clashed for decades with Myanmar's army. Now, high-end SUVs thunder past trucks carrying building materials and workers.

The Kaung Kha militia's immaculate and expansive new headquarters sits on a plateau nestled between the steep green hills of the jagged Loi Sam Sip range. About six kilometers away, near Loikan village, is a sprawling drug facility carved out of thick forests. Police and locals say the complex churns out vast quantities of crystal meth, heroin, ketamine and yaba tablets - a cheaper form of meth that is mixed with caffeine. It was raided in early 2018 and security forces seized more than 200,000 litres of precursor chemicals, as well as 10,000 kg of caffeine and 73,550 kg of sodium hydroxide - all substances used in drug production.

According to a Yangon-based AFP officer, the Loikan facility was "very likely" to have been the source of much of the Sam Gor syndicate's meth. In a reported interview, Oi Khun, a communications officer for the 3,000-strong Kaung Kha militia said, "Some militia were involved in the lab." He paused, then added: "But not with the knowledge of senior members of the militia".

One person in Loikan described how workers from the lab would come down from the hills. These men, like most of the villagers, were ethnic Chinese. But they dressed better than the locals, had foreign accents, and had a foul smell about them. Meth lab managers and chemists are mostly Taiwan nationals. So, too, are many of the crime network's couriers and boat crews who transport the drugs across the Asia-Pacific.

Shan's super-labs produce the purest crystal meth in the world. "They can take it slow and spread (the meth) out on the ground and let it dry."

According to UNODC estimates, the Asia-Pacific retail market for meth in 2019 was worth between $ 30.3 and $ 61.4 billion annually. The business model for meth is "very different" to heroin, said one UNODC officer. "Inputs are relatively cheap, a large workforce is not needed, the price per kilo is higher, and profits are therefore far, far higher."

The wholesale price of a kilo of crystal meth produced in northeastern Myanmar is as little as $ 1,800, according to a UNODC report citing the China National Narcotics Control Commission. Average retail prices for crystal meth, according to the UN agency, are equivalent to $ 70,500 per kilo in Thailand, $ 298,000 per kilo in Australia and $ 588,000 in Japan. For the Japanese market, that's more than a three-hundred-fold mark-up.

According to experts, in this region, organized crime have all the ingredients in-place that they need to continue to grow the business, including territory to produce, access to chemicals, established trafficking routes and relationships to move product, and a massive population with spending power to target

The enormous money the syndicate is making means that even if they lose ten tons and only one goes through, they still make a big profit. They can afford failure and seizures. It doesn't matter.

The analysis of Cai's phones was continuously providing leads. On them, police found the GPS coordinates of the pick-up point in the Andaman Sea where fishing boats laden with Myanmar meth were meeting drug mother ships capable of remaining at sea for weeks.

One of the mother ships was a Taiwanese trawler called the Shun de Man 66. The vessel was already at sea, when in early July 2017, Joshua Joseph Smith walked into a marine broker in the Western Australian capital of Perth and paid $A 350,000 (about $ 265,000 at that time) for the MV Valkoista, a fishing charter boat. Smith, who was in his mid-40s and hailed from the east coast of Australia, inquired about sea sickness tablets. According to local media, he didn't have a fishing license at the time.

After buying the boat on 7 July 2017, Smith set the Valkoista on a course straight from the marina to meet the Shun De Man 66 in the Indian Ocean. After the rendezvous, the Valkoista then sailed to the remote Western Australian port city of Geraldton. On 11 July 2017, its crew were seen "unloading a lot of packages" into a van.

According to some police officials, "We knew we had an importation. We know the methodology of organized crime networks. We know if a ship leaves empty and comes back with some gear on it, that it hasn't just dropped from the sky in the middle of the ocean."

Investigators checked CCTV footage and hotel, plane and car rental records. The phones of some of the Australian drug traffickers were tapped. It soon became apparent that some of Smith's alleged co-conspirators were members of an ethnic Lebanese underworld gang, as well as the Hells Angels and Comanchero motorcycle gangs, known as "bikies" in Australia.

Smith's associates met with Sam Gor syndicate members in Bangkok in August 2017 to put together their deal to import 1.2 tonnes of crystal meth into Australia. The Australians reconvened in Perth a month later.

Bikers have a reputation for wild clubhouse parties and a self-styled mythology as outsiders, but they have refined tastes. They fly business class, stay in five-star hotels and dine at the finest restaurants. One of these restaurants is the Rockpool Bar & Grill in Perth - a unique steakhouse, combining an impressive dining room, an open kitchen with its signature wood fire grill. The restaurant offers a 104-page wine list offering 2300 different wines and a menu that includes caviar with toast at about $ 185 per serving.

On 27 November 2017, the Shun De Man 66 set sail again, this time from Singapore. The vessel headed north into the Andaman Sea to rendezvous with a smaller boat bringing the meth from Myanmar. The Shun De Man then sailed along the west coast of the Indonesian island of Sumatra and dropped down to the Indian Ocean.

The Indonesian Navy watched and the AFP listened.

When the Shun De Man finally again met the Valkoista in international waters off the West Australian coast on 19 December 2017, the investigators heard an Asian voice shouting "money, money." The Shun De Man's crew had one half of a torn Hong Kong dollar bill. Smith and his crew had the other half. The Australian buyers proved their identity by matching their portion to the fragment held by the crew of the Shun De Man, who then handed over the meth.

The Valkoista arrived in the Australian port city of Geraldton following a two-day return journey in rough seas. The men unloaded the drugs in the pre-dawn dark. Masked members of the AFP and Western Australian police moved in with assault weapons and seized the drugs and arrested the men. Smith pleaded guilty to importing commercial quantity of an illegal drug. Some of his alleged associates are still on trial.

Taiwan's Ministry of Justice Investigation Bureau said it had "worked together with our counterparts on the investigation" of the Shun De Man 66 and that this had led to the "substantial seizure of illicit narcotics" by the Australian authorities in December 2017. The bureau said it was "aware that Taiwanese syndicates have participated in maritime drug trafficking in (the) Asia-Pacific region," and was working "collaboratively and closely with our counterparts to disrupt these syndicates and cross-border drug trafficking."

In the words of one investigator, the syndicate's supply chain is so complex and expertly run that it "must rival Apple's." According to Jay Li Chien-chih, a Taiwanese police senior colonel who had been stationed in Southeast Asia for a decade, "The syndicate has a lot of money and there is a vast market to tap….. "The power this network possesses is unimaginable."

Investigators have had successes. In February 2018, police busted the Loikan super-lab in Myanmar, where they found enough tea-branded packaging for 10 tonnes of meth. The Shun De Man 66 was intercepted that month by the Indonesian navy with more than one tonne of meth aboard. In March 2018, a key Sam Gor lieutenant was arrested in Cambodia and extradited to Myanmar.

In December 2018, the house of Sue Songkittikul, a suspected syndicate operations chief, was raided in Thailand. Located near the border with Myanmar, the moat-ringed compound had a small meth lab, which police suspected was used to experiment with new recipes; a powerful radio tower with a 100-km range; and an underground tunnel from the main house to the back of the property.

Sue Songkittikul wasn't there, but property and money from 38 bank accounts linked to him totaling some $ 9 million were seized during the investigation. Sue is still at large.

But the flow of drugs leaving the Golden Triangle for the wider Asia-Pacific seems to have increased. Seizures of crystal meth and yaba rose about 50% last year to 126 tonnes in East and Southeast Asia. At the same time, prices for the drugs fell in most countries. This pattern of falling prices and rising seizures, the UNODC said in a report released in March 2019, "suggested the supply of the drug had expanded."

Quarterly data from both East and Southeast Asia show a drop in seizures in the second quarter of 2020 during the height of the pandemic. However, seizures quickly rebounded from the third quarter onwards, demonstrating the flexibility of organized crime groups to adapt to change and take advantage of porous borders in the region. Wholesale prices of crystalline methamphetamine declined in several countries in Southeast Asia, namely Cambodia, Malaysia, and Thailand, while its purity remained stable, indicating limited impact on the availability of methamphetamine.

A record amount of methamphetamine – nearly 172 tons – was seized in East and Southeast Asia in 2021, with over 1 billion methamphetamine tablets recorded for the first time. The total is seven times higher than it was 10 years ago, when just more than 143 million tablets were seized, and over thirty-five times higher than it was close to 20 years ago. Nearly 79 tons of crystal methamphetamine was also seized in 2021– approximately eight times the 10 tons seized a decade ago.

The supply of Golden Triangle methamphetamine also expanded further into South Asia in 2021. Crystal methamphetamine in distinct Golden Triangle packaging and tablets were increasingly seized in northeastern India, in a pattern similar to Bangladesh a few years ago.

The price of both tablet and crystal methamphetamine also continues to drop across Southeast Asia. Malaysia and Thailand have reported that wholesale and street prices had decreased to all-time lows in 2021 as the supply surged. "The drop in the price of crystal methamphetamine is particularly concerning, as it has become much more accessible and available to those who could not afford it before. The social consequences of increased use are significant, and health and harm reduction services remain limited across the region," observed Kavinvadee Suppapongtevasakul, UNODC regional synthetic drugs analyst for the Global SMART Programme.

Although methamphetamine is the primary concern of authorities across the region, other synthetic drugs notably ketamine are also widely available,.

The Sam Gor syndicate is a nimble and elusive adversary. When authorities had successes stopping the drug motherships, Sam Gor syndicate switched to hiding its product in shipping containers. When Thailand stopped much of the meth coming directly across the border from Myanmar by truck, the syndicate re-routed deliveries through Laos and Vietnam. This included deploying hoardes of Laotians with backpacks, each containing about 30 kilos of meth, to carry it into Thailand through narrow jungle paths.

According to a BBC report, Australian police had been tracking Tse Chi Lop for 10 years before his arrest at Amsterdam's Schiphol airport on 22 January 2021, from where he was preparing to fly to Canada. Dutch police acted on a request by the AFP, after an arrest warrant and Interpol Red Diffusion notice was issued. "He was already on the most-wanted list and he was detained based on intelligence we received," Dutch police spokesperson Thomas Aling said.

The Australian police wanted Tse Chi Lop to face trial in Australia and wanted his extradition. In June 2021, a Dutch court approved Australia's request for extradition. Tse appealed to the Supreme Court against the extradition decision.

Tse denies he is a kingpin and claims his arrest was effectively set up by Australian authorities, alleging they illegally arranged for his expulsion from Taiwan to Canada to include a stop in the Netherlands so that he could be arrested there. In June 2022, the Supreme Court of Netherland dismissed the appeal. The Court held that Tse can be extradited to Australia. Tse has been extradited to Australia in December 2022 to face his trial there.

Tse headed the Sam Gor Syndicate which dominates a $ 70 bn illegal drugs market across Asia. The 58-year-old has been compared to the Mexican drug lord Joaquin "El Chapo" Guzman because of the scale of his alleged enterprise.

UN estimates that the syndicate's revenue from methamphetamine sales alone could have been as high as $ 17 bn in 2018. Tse is married to a woman known as Tse Yim Fum. No further details are available about the wife.

Meanwhile, Lee Chung Chak, 66, reputed to be second in command of Sam Gor was arrested by Thai Narcotics Police on 1 October 2020 based on an arrest warrant issued by a Thai court, following an extradition request by the Australian authorities. In June 2022, the Australian agencies succeeded in getting Lee Chung Chak, extradited from Thailand. He is undergoing trial in Australia.

With Tse and Lee, the top two out of the picture, the hierarchy and structure of the Sam Gor syndicate has been shaken. But someone else will certainly take over and the business will continue as before.

The Golden Crescent

The Golden Crescent is one of Asia's two illicit opium production areas. The other being the Golden Triangle. The Golden Crescent is located at the crossroads of Central, South, and Western Asia. This space overlaps three nations - Afghanistan, Iran, and Pakistan, whose mountainous peripheries define the crescent.

The Golden Crescent has a much older history of opium production than Southeast Asia's Golden Triangle. The Golden Triangle emerged as a modern-day opium-producing entity in the 1980s. Afghanistan began producing opium in significant quantities in the mid-1950s, almost 3 decades ago, to supply opium to its neighbor Iran after poppy cultivation was banned there. In the mid-1970s, political instability combined with a prolonged drought disrupted supplies from the Golden Triangle. Afghanistan and Pakistan increased their production and became major suppliers of opiates to Western Europe and North America. In the 1980s, the Golden Triangle began making an impact on the opium and morphine market. In order to meet the increasing demand, the Golden Triangle has steadily increased its output since then. In 1991, Afghanistan became the world's primary opium producer, with a yield of 1,782 metric tons (U.S. State Department estimates), surpassing Myanmar, formerly the world leader in opium production. The Soviet–Afghan War was a conflict wherein insurgent groups (collectively known as the Afghan Mujahideen), as well as smaller Maoist groups, fought a nine-year guerrilla war against the Soviet Army and the Democratic Republic of Afghanistan government throughout the 1980s, mostly in the Afghan countryside. The Mujahideen were variously backed by U.S., Pakistan, Iran, Saudi Arabia, China, and the United Kingdom. During the American-led invasion of Afghanistan in 2001, in retaliation to the September 11th terrorist attacks, the Golden Crescent's opium production took a huge hit, producing almost 90% less opium than in

2000.

At the peak of its opium production, in 2007 the Golden Crescent produced more than 8,000 of the world's total of about 9,000 tons of opium, a near monopoly. The Golden Crescent also dominates the cannabis resin market due to the high resin yields of the region (145 kg/ha), four times more than Morocco (36 kg/ha). The Golden Crescent also caters to a much larger market - about 64% more than the Golden Triangle. It produces and distributes over 2,500 tons of opiates to Africa, Europe, the Americas and Central Asia and supplies to almost 9.5 million opiate users worldwide.

Taliban

The Taliban, literally meaning 'students' or 'seekers', is a Deobandi Islamist religious-political movement and military organization in Afghanistan, regarded by many governments and organizations as terrorists. It is one of two entities claiming to be the legitimate government of Afghanistan, alongside the internationally recognized Islamic Republic of Afghanistan.

The Taliban are a movement of religious students (talib) from the Pashtun areas of eastern and southern Afghanistan who were educated in traditional Islamic schools in Pakistan. In September 1994, Mullah Mohammad Omar founded the group in his home town of Kandahar with 50 students. In 1994, the Taliban emerged as one of the prominent factions in the Afghan Civil War and largely consisted of students (talib) from the Pashtun areas of eastern and southern Afghanistan who had been educated in traditional Islamic schools, and fought during the Soviet–Afghan War. Under the leadership of Mohammed Omar, the movement spread throughout most of Afghanistan, shifting power away from the Mujahideen warlords. Mohammed Omar remained the Supreme Commander of the Taliban till his death in 2013.

On 3 November 1994, in a surprise attack, the Taliban conquered Kandahar City. By 4 January 1995, they controlled 12 Afghan provinces. The totalitarian Islamic Emirate of Afghanistan was established in 1996 and the Afghan capital was transferred to Kandahar. When the Taliban took power in 1996, twenty years of continuous warfare had devastated entire Afghanistan's infrastructure and economy. From 1996 to 2001, the Taliban held power over roughly three-quarters of Afghanistan. They enforced a strict interpretation of Sharia, or Islamic law, until overthrown by the American-led invasion of Afghanistan in December 2001 following the September 11 attacks.

The decrease in heroin production from Myanmar was the result of several years of unfavorable growing conditions and new government policies of forced eradication. During the same time frame, Afghan heroin production increased, with a notable decrease in 2001 allegedly as a result of Taliban's fatwa against heroin production. Taliban banned poppy growing in 2000 as they sought international legitimacy. But according to experts, they faced a popular backlash and later changed their stance. Afghanistan produced over 90% of the world's illicit opium. In addition to opiates, Afghanistan was also the world's largest producer of hashish.

U.S. spent more than $ 8 bn over 15 years on efforts to deprive Taliban of their profits from Afghanistan's opium and heroin trade - from poppy eradication to air attacks and raids on suspected labs. That strategy failed. In August 2021, U.S. wrapped up its longest war. Afghanistan remained the world's biggest illicit opiate supplier and looks certain to remain so as Taliban has taken over power in Kabul.

Afghan farmers weigh several factors in deciding how much poppy to plant. These range from annual precipitation, and the price of wheat, the main alternative crop to poppy, to world opium and heroin prices.

Yet even during droughts and wheat shortages, when wheat prices have rocketed, Afghan farmers have grown poppy and extracted opium gum that is refined into morphine and heroin. In recent years, many farmers have installed Chinese-made solar panels to power deep water wells.

According to the UNODC, three of the last four years have seen some of Afghanistan's highest levels of opium production. Even as the COVID-19 pandemic raged, in 2020 poppy cultivation soared 37 percent. According to Barnett Rubin, a former US Department of

State adviser on Afghanistan, illicit narcotics are "the country's largest industry except for war".

The estimated all-time high opium production was reached in 2017 at 9,900 tons worth some $ 1.4 bn in sales by farmers or roughly 7 percent of Afghanistan's GDP, the UNODC reported. When the value of drugs for export and local consumption is taken into account, along with imported precursor chemicals, UNODC has estimated the country's overall illicit opiate economy that year at around $ 6.6 bn.

Hajji Bashir Noorzai

It is rather surprising that hardly anyone in Afghanistan has been convicted of drug related charges. A notable exception is Hajji Bashir Noorzai - a former Afghan drug lord. Initially, he was a supporter of the Taliban movement and a close confidant of late Taliban founder Mullah Mohammad Omar. He fought the Soviet forces that occupied Afghanistan from 1979 to 1989. After Mohammad Omar went into hiding, Noorzai was left in charge of Kandahar. Noorzai provided explosives, weapons, and militia fighters to the Taliban regime.

Noorzai was in Quetta when the 11 September 2001 attacks occurred. He returned to Afghanistan soon afterwards. In November 2001, he met with men he described as American military officials at Spinboldak, near the Afghan-Pakistani border. Small teams of U.S. Special Forces and intelligence officers were in Afghanistan at the time, seeking the support of tribal leaders. According to his lawyer, Noorzai was taken to Kandahar, where he was detained and questioned by the Americans for six days about Taliban officials and operations. He agreed to work with them and was freed. In late January 2002, he handed over 15 truckloads of weapons, including about 400 anti-aircraft missiles that had been hidden by the Taliban in his tribe's territory. On 1 June 2004, the U.S. State Department sanctioned Noorzai under the Foreign Narcotics Kingpin Designation Act and placed his name in a list of the most wanted drug lords in the world.

Despite being among America's most wanted drug traffickers, after he was assured by his handlers that he would not be arrested, he agreed to go to New York City for a debriefing. But ten days after his arrival in New York, he was arrested.

In April 2005, U.S. authorities in New York City arrested Noorzai. He was charged with trying to smuggle more than US $ 50 million worth of heroin into the U.S In his trial in 2008, Noorzai was represented by New York high-profile criminal defense lawyer Ivan Fisher. The case has raised substantial questions about U.S. foreign policy abroad. In 2008, Noorzai was convicted of smuggling $ 50 million worth of heroin into the U.S. On 30 April 2009, Judge Denny Chin sentenced Noorzai to life imprisonment. The new Taliban government wanted him back. In September 2022, U.S. freed him in a prisoner swap (exchange) of Mark Frerichs, a US Navy veteran who had been held captive in Afghanistan since 2020.

Haji Juma Khan, another drug lord, suddenly rose to national prominence after the American-led invasion of Afghanistan. He was briefly detained by American forces after the 2001 fall of the Taliban, but released, even though American officials knew that he was involved in narcotics trafficking. He took over the drug business after the arrest of Noorzai. In 2008, he was detained in Indonesia for unknown reasons and transported to New York. Sometime in April 2018, he was quietly released without any pending charges or a trial.

The Medellin And The Cali Drug Cartels

For almost quarter of a century, Colombia had two main drug cartels – the Medellin and the Cali drug cartels.

The Medellin cartel derived its name from the City of Medellin – capital of Antioquia province, about 23 kilometers from Bogota. The founder Godfather of the Medellin cartel (killed on 2 December 1993) was Pablo Escobar Gaviria.

Escobar started as a small time crook in his childhood days and rapidly rose to power by ruthlessly kidnapping and killing his enemies. He built the Medellin cartel in 1976 and cultivated a Robin Hood image for himself, providing jobs, interest free loans, and houses to the local people.

In April 1983, the Medellin river flooded its banks destroying the shacks of several hundred rag pickers. A week later, Escobar arrived there and promised new houses to the homeless. The next month, 360 families moved into new homes with plumbing, electricity and gardens, in 'Barrio Pablo Escobar' situated on a hill above the city. These families had to pay only for the electricity and water. So rich are the drug traffickers, that in 1984, they offered to clear off the country's entire debts in return for amnesty. The Government refused the offer.

The Cali cartel derived its name from the city of Cali which is situated on the Cali river in western Colombia. It is older than the city of Medellin. The Cali cartel was a loose bunch of drug traffickers founded by Gilberto Rodriguez Orezuela, a banker by profession; his brother Miguel, an attorney; and a third brother José Santacruz Londoño.

The Role of the U.S.

U.S. was the main sufferer of this illegal drug trade because 80% of the cocaine from Colombia and other Latin American countries found its way into the U.S. The U.S. Government had been providing substantial funds to the drug producing and supplying countries for anti-drug activities. But the Medellin and Cali cartels were extremely powerful and ruthless. They offered huge bribes, and in case of refusal, simply eliminated those who came in their way. Demoralized by corruption and virtually paralyzed with fear, the Colombian courts were not willing to support or continue the fight against the powerful drug traffickers. Every conviction was followed by retaliatory murder. No wonder, even the Supreme Court refused to implement the U.S. – Colombia Extradition Treaty.

On 18 January 1989, the Medellin cartel massacred all the twelve members of a Judicial Commission which had come to Barrancabermeja to make some investigations. On 16 August 1989, they murdered a Bogota Superior Criminal Court Judge, Carlos Henrique Valencia Garcia, after he had signed the arrest order of the Medellin drug trafficker Gonzalo Rodriguez Gacha who was accused of murdering the left wing politician Jaime Pardo Leal in October 1987.

On 18 August 1989, the police chief Col. Valdemar Franlin, who had organized successful raids on the Medellin cartel's drug producing centers was murdered.

On the same day was also murdered Luis Carlos Galan Sarmineto, regarded as the future President, because of his outspoken condemnation of the domination of the country's political and economical life by the major drug traffickers. The Medellin cartel had issued $ 5,00,000 death warrant (supari) for his murder.

The spate of murders led President Vergilio Barco Vargas to declare a number of emergency measures which amounted to a virtual crackdown on the Medellin cartel. He appealed to the U.S. President for increased aid. President George Bush immediately responded with an emergency military package totaling $ 65,000,000. Escobar hit back. He announced a reward of $ 4,000 to any one killing a police officer and threatened to kill 10 judges for every drug trafficker they ordered to be deported to the U.S.

On 15 December 1989, Colombia police's anti-narcotics squad shot dead Gonzalo Rodriguez Gacha, the military chief of the Medellin cartel, 600 kilometers north of Bogota.

On 11 August 1990, Colombian security forces shot dead Gustavo de Jesus Gaviria Rivero, then head of the Medellin cartel (because the real leader and Gustavo's cousin Pablo Escobar Gaviria was in hiding) in the town of Medellin.

In a bid to stop the mad spate of killings, on 8 October 1990, the Colombian Government offered the drug traffickers a guarantee that if they surrendered voluntarily, they would not be extradited to the U.S. and their sentences would be considerably reduced. Between 1989 and 1991, Colombia arrested and deported 26 cartel members to the U.S. But on 19 January 1991, the Colombian Congress repealed the law permitting the extradition of drug traffickers and the new Constitution which came into effect on 5 July 1991 banned extradition.

Escobar surrendered in 1991, but on his own terms. He would not be deported to the U.S. and would be kept in a jail built to his specifications, ostensibly for his safety and security. The jail specially built for him had a swimming pool, a tennis court, a sauna, telephones, fax and his personal security personnel. Actually, Escobar controlled his drug empire from this so called prison.

The term Narco-terrorism itself was coined by former President Fernando Belaúnde Terry of Peru in 1983 when describing terrorist-type attacks against his nation's anti-narcotics police. Narco-terrorism, in its original context, referred to the attempts of narcotics traffickers to influence the policies of a government or a society through violence and intimidation, and to hinder the enforcement of anti-drug laws by the systematic threat or use of such violence.

During the 1984 –1993 period, Colombia was known as one of the countries that suffered a number of terrorist attacks waged by narcotic traffickers like Pablo Escobar on the Colombian government. On 30 April 1984, a motorcycle gunman from the Medellin Cartel killed Rodrigo Lara Bonilla, the Minister of Justice.

On 6 November 1985, at 11:35 a.m., three vehicles carrying 35 guerrillas (25 men and 10 women) stormed the Palace of Justice of Colombia, entering through the basement. Meanwhile, another group of guerrillas disguised as civilians took over the first floor and the main entrance. The guerrillas killed security guards Eulogio Blanco and Gerardo Díaz Arbeláez and the building manager Jorge Tadeo Mayo Castro. The official report judged that the guerrillas planned the takeover operation to be a 'bloody takeover'. According to the official sources, the guerrillas "set out to shoot indiscriminately and detonate building-shaking bombs while chanting M19-praising battle cries."

The M-19 lost one guerrilla and a nurse during the initial raid on the building. After the guerrillas had neutralized the security personnel guarding the building, they installed armed posts at strategic places, such as the stairs and the fourth floor. A group of guerrillas led by Commander Luis Otero got up to the fourth floor and kidnapped Chief Justice Alfonso Reyes Echandía, President of the Supreme Court. In the meantime, many hostages took refuge in empty offices on the first floor, where they hid until around 2 pm.

The assailants took hostage 300 people, including the 24 justices and 20 other judges. The first hostage the guerrilla group asked for was the Supreme Court Justice and President of the Constitutional Court, then called Sala Constitucional, Manuel Gaona Cruz, who was in charge of delivering the decision of the court with regard to the constitutionality of the extradition treaty between Colombia and the U.S. About three hours after the initial seizure, army troops rescued about 200 hostages from the lower three floors of the building and the surviving gunmen and remaining hostages occupying the upper two floors.

The M-19 members demanded via telephone that President Belisario Betancur should come to the Palace of Justice in order to negotiate. The President refused. The retaking of the building began that day and ended on 7 November 1985 when Army troops stormed the Palace of Justice and took over.

Colonel Alfonso Plazas Vega, commander of an armored cavalry battalion, personally oversaw the operations. The siege of the Palace of Justice and the subsequent raid was one of the deadliest attacks in Colombia in its war with leftist rebels. 98 persons died. In 2010, retired Colonel Alfonso Plazas Vega was sentenced to 30 years of jail time for his alleged role in forced disappearances after the siege. However, on 16 December 2015, in a five to three vote, Colonel Plazas Vega was declared innocent by the Colombian Supreme Court and absolved of his previous 30 year prison sentence.

Avianca Flight 203 was a Colombian domestic passenger flight from El Dorado International Airport in Bogotá to Alfonso Bonilla Aragón International Airport in Cali, Colombia. The aircraft was a Boeing 727-21 built in 1966. On 27 November 1989, it was blown up by plastic explosives over the municipality of Soacha. All 107 people on board as well as 3 people on the ground were killed. The bombing had been ordered by Drug kingpin Pablo Escobar of the Medellín drug cartel to kill César Gaviria Trujillo, the Presidential candidate of the 1990 elections. Fortunately, César Gaviria Trujillo was not in the flight. He survived and won the elections to become the President.

The Cali cartel wanted to finish off Escobar. In 1989, they hired Jorge Salcedo Cabrera, a civil engineer, to help them assassinate Pablo Escobar. Salcedo had previously worked on behalf of British commandos, who worked with the Colombian government to counter the Revolutionary Armed Forces of Colombia. They hired Salcedo because in the past he had befriended and hired a group of mercenaries to wage war against the left-wing guerrilla forces in an operation sanctioned by Colombia's military. The mercenary group was made up of 12 former special operations soldiers, including the British Special Air Service. Salcedo felt it was his patriotic duty and accepted the deal to bring the mercenaries back to Colombia and help plan the operation to kill Pablo Escobar. The group of British ex-soldiers accepted the offer. The Cali cartel provided food, housing and weapons to the mercenaries.

Salcedo had planned to attack Escobar at his Hacienda Nápoles compound. They trained for a few months till they heard Escobar was going to be staying at the compound, celebrating the victory of his football team. They planned to enter the compound by using two heavily armed Hughes 500 armed helicopters and kill Escobar during the early morning. To confuse onlookers, they painted the helicopters to look like police helicopters. They took off and headed towards the compound but one of the helicopters crashed onto a mountainside, minutes away from the compound. The pilot was killed during the crash. The plan was aborted and they had to conduct a rescue mission up the dense mountainside.

The second plot to kill Escobar was to bomb the prison by using an A-37 Dragonfly surplus ground-attack jet bomber in private ownership. The Cali Cartel had a connection in El Salvador - a general of El Salvador's military who illegally sold them four 500-pound bombs for about half a million dollars.

Salcedo flew over to El Salvador to oversee the plan to pick up the bombs and take them to an airfield where a civilian jet would land to pick them up and take them to Colombia. But when the jet landed at the airfield, they found that it was a small executive jet. They attempted to load the four bombs, and what was planned to take a few minutes, took them over 20 minutes. By this time, a crowd of civilians had gathered at the airfield curious to know what was happening. Only three bombs could fit in the small passenger cabin. The jet took off. Salcedo abandoned the fourth bomb and went back to his hotel. The morning after, the activities of the previous night were all over the news. Salcedo barely escaped El Salvador and arrest before the botched pickup was exposed. Law enforcement agencies had discovered the bomb and some of the people involved in the operation were arrested. They told the authorities about the plot to kill Escobar with the bombs.

In 1992, when Escobar's trial was about to begin, the Government wanted to transfer him to an ordinary prison. He did not agree. Government intermediaries tried to persuade him, but he refused and literally walked away.

Escobar had amassed a lot of wealth. Forbes magazine rated him as the richest man in the world from 1989 to 1991 with a personal wealth of about $ 3 billion in 1989. He even had two submarines and a fleet of small private airplanes for his business.

On 2 December 1993, with $ 8.7 million on his head, Escobar was surrounded by 500 police officers and soldiers and shot dead. Thousands of mourners mourned his death. He had become a celebrity in his native place – donating liberally to charities, building homes for the poor and encouraging soccer. Escobar's death virtually marked the end of the supremacy of the Medellin cartel. The Cali cartel took over 80% of the drug business in Colombia.

Pablo Escobar lived in the building known as Monaco – actually a fortified eight-story concrete block with a penthouse, in El Poblado district, one of Medellin's poshiest areas, for several years till 1988, when rivals bombed it. The Escobar family abandoned the building, and it remained vacant for more than 25 years after Escobar's death.

The Monaco building was a popular tourist attraction. Escobar the "cocaine king" was remembered by many in Colombia as something of a Robin Hood figure because of his charity, and the distribution of part of his vast wealth to Medellin's poor.

According to some officials, between 1983 and 1994, Colombia's drug violence resulted in the killing of 46,612 people, with Escobar at the center of most of it. Since 2018, visitors to the building had been confronted by posters that informed them of the grim tally of deaths that included civilians, police, journalists, and judges.

The Government of Colombia wanted to bring out the darker side of Medellin's violent past in the foreground, telling the stories of victims. This involved demolishing Monaco building.

"It's not about erasing history but telling the story from the right side; that of the victims and the innocent heroes," Medellin's city hall tweeted.

On 22 February 2019, the Monaco building was razed to the ground with explosives in a public show for a crowd of around 1,600 people including families of some of Escobar's victims as part of an effort to change the way the drug lord's story is told.

Colombian President Ivan Duque flew down to Medellin to see the demolition, saying the demolition "signifies the defeat of the culture of illegality."

"It signifies that history won't be written from the perpetrator's perspective".

The Colombian Government plans to turn the property into a commemorative space to remember victims of the drug trade who were killed during the 1980s and 1990s in a bloody war with the authorities.

Hacienda Nápoles and the hippos

Escobar had extravagant and exquisite taste. He created or bought numerous residences and safe houses, with the Hacienda Nápoles being the most amazing. This luxury house contained a colonial house, a sculpture park, and a complete zoo with animals from various continents, including elephants, exotic birds, giraffes, and even hippopotamuses. Escobar had planned to construct a Greek-style citadel near it. Although construction of the citadel was started, it was never finished.

After Escobar's death, the government gave the ranch, zoo and citadel at Hacienda Nápoles to low-income families under a law called Extinción de Dominio (Domain Extinction). The property has been converted into a theme park surrounded by four luxury hotels overlooking the zoo.

Escobar had imported four hippos in his private zoo at Hacienda Nápoles. After Escobar's death, they were considered to be too difficult to seize and move. They were left on the untended estate. By 2007, the hippos had multiplied to 16 and had taken to roaming in the nearby Magdalena River area for food. In 2009, two adults and one calf escaped the herd and after attacking humans and killing cattle, one of the adults (called "Pepe") was killed by hunters under authorization from the local authorities. As of early 2014, 40 hippos have been reported to exist in Puerto Triunfo, Antioquia. In 2021, the number of hippos had increased to around 80. A number of hippos may have to be culled.

A number of books have been written about Escobar. The Netflix series *Narcos* has become a huge hit. The stories and movies on Escobar have actually glorified the drug lord's life.

Ernesto Samper Pizano who was President of Colombia from 1994 to 1998, stated that his government would re-examine the policy of offering lenient terms of surrender to cartel leaders as the most expeditious way of curbing the drug trade. He announced the appointment of a commission to make recommendations to ensure that the justice system dealt adequately with the drug traffickers. Since 1994, U.S. has been spending a lot of money in aerial fumigation and manual destruction of the coca crops in Colombia. But fumigation planes were destroyed. Manual eradication turned out to be quite dangerous. A large number of eradicators, or their escorts in the security forces, were killed by ambushes, snipers, landmines, and improvised explosive devices hidden among the coca plants. Hundreds more were wounded.

In 2000, U.S. began funding of Plan Colombia, aimed at eradicating drug crops and taking action against drug lords accused of engaging in narco terrorism. This continued under the U.S. Bush administration. U.S. was not happy with the state of affairs in Colombia. In his report to the Congress and to the American people, the President noted with serious concern that a decision of the Supreme Court had virtually legalized the use and possession of user amounts of some drugs creating a dangerous climate for the health and well being of Colombian citizens; that the Colombian Government had not arrested or prosecuted any leader of the drug cartels; that there continued to be talks of lenient plea bargaining agreements; that little action had been taken to force the traffickers to relinquish their illicit gains; and worse, the Colombian Government was not able to guarantee the safety of witnesses and their families, or to make effective use of evidence supplied by the U.S. The U.S. Government, therefore, suspended the sharing of evidence with Colombian Government in new drug cases.

Rise and fall of the Cali Cartel

The Cali Cartel was formed in the 1970s, around the city of Cali and the Valle del Cauca Department. The group originally assembled as a ring of kidnappers known as "Las Chemas", led by Luis Fernando Tamayo García. Las Chemas were implicated in numerous kidnappings, including those of two Swiss citizens - a diplomat, Herman Buff, and a student, Zack "Jazz Milis" Martin. The kidnappers reportedly received $ 700,000 in ransom, which is believed to have been used to fund their drug trafficking empire.

The Las Chemas group first involved itself in trafficking marijuana. Due to the product's low profit rate and large amounts required to traffic to cover resources, the fledgling group decided to shift their focus to cocaine - a more lucrative drug. In the early 1970s, the cartel sent Hélmer Herrera to New York City to establish a distribution center, during a time when the United States Drug Enforcement Administration (DEA) viewed cocaine as less important than heroin.

The founders of Cali Cartel were three brothers - Gilberto Rodríguez Orejuela, Miguel Rodríguez Orejuela and José Santacruz Londoño. In the late 1980s, they broke away from Pablo Escobar and his Medellín associates. When Hélmer "Pacho" Herrera joined the group, it became a four-man executive board that ran the cartel.

It is believed a hired assassin attempted to kill Herrera while he was attending a sports event. The gunman opened fire using a machine gun on the crowd where Herrera was sitting, killing 19. However, he did not hit Herrera. Herrera is believed to have been a founding member of Los Pepes, a group which operated alongside authorities with the intention of killing or capturing Pablo Escobar.

The Cali Cartel operated as a tight group of independent criminal organizations, as opposed to the Medellíns' centralized structure under leader Pablo Escobar. According to the then DEA chief Thomas Constantine, the Cali Cartel eventually became "The biggest, most powerful crime syndicate we've ever known",

Its members worked more like respectable businessmen. The Cali group was nicknamed "Los Caballeros de Cali" ("Gentlemen of Cali"). The Cali Cartel was less violent than its Medellin counterpart.

There have been inter-rival feuds between the Medellin and the Cali drug cartels involving numerous ruthless killings. At the height of the feuds, there were 10 to 15 killings every day.

After the elimination of Escobar, the Cali Cartel became the number one. At the height of their reign from 1993-1995, Cali Cartel controlled over 80% of the world's cocaine market and were directly responsible for the growth of the cocaine market in Europe, controlling 80% of the market there as well. By the mid-1990s, the Cali Cartel's international drug trafficking empire was a $ 7 billion a year criminal enterprise. The Cali Cartel made several innovations in trafficking and production. It moved its refining operations out of Colombia to Peru and Bolivia. It pioneered new trafficking routes through Panama. Cali Cartel also diversified into opium and was reported to have brought in a Japanese chemist to help its refining operation. Gilberto was able to become the Chairman of the Board of Banco de Trabajadores. This bank is believed to have been used to launder funds for the Cali Cartel, as well as of Pablo Escobar's Medellín Cartel.

On 4 June 1995, the Colombian Police arrested Santa Cruz London, a founder member of the Cali Cartel, and the third most important Cali Cartel leader.

On 9 June 1995, they arrested Gilberto Rodriguez Orezuela, an important member of the Cali Cartel. Several other important members surrendered. Both the Medellin and Cali Cartels were virtually destroyed. But small timers came up and took over the trade. In July 1996, a female U.S. Drug Enforcement Agency informant in the Cali Cartel, code-named 'Maria' deposed before the U.S. Senate Committee on Foreign Relations that even though six Cali Cartel leaders were locked up in jails in Colombia in 1995, the Cali Cartel had not been liquidated. The leaders continued to control the business from inside the jail. She further stated that President Ernesto Samper Pizano had contacts with the Cali Cartel and had taken money from them. However, in 1996, the Colombian Congress cleared President Ernesto Samper Pizano of drug-related corruption charges.

Extradition had been banned in Colombia under the 1991

Constitution. On 23 October 1996, a Senate Committee of Colombia approved a proposed constitutional amendment to reintroduce extradition of Colombian nationals wanted for trial in other countries. This amendment was made under pressure from the U.S. On 17 January 1997, a Cali court sentenced the two brothers - Miguel and Gilberto Rodrigues Orejuela, of the Cali Cartel who were arrested in 1995, to 8 and 10 years imprisonment respectively, on charges of drug trafficking, illicit enrichment and conspiracy. They received reduction in their sentences for confessing, and for submitting to Colombia's plea bargaining laws. They could get further reduction of fifty percent of the sentences for working in jail. Gilberto and Miguel were extradited to the U.S. in 2006. On 26 September 2006, both pleaded guilty in a court in Miami, Florida, to charges of conspiracy to import cocaine into the U.S. Upon their confession, they agreed to forfeit $ 2.1 billion in assets. The agreement, however, did not require them to co-operate in other investigations. They were solely responsible for identification of the assets stemming from their cocaine trafficking. Colombian officials raided and seized the Drogas la Rebaja pharmacy chain, replacing 50 of its 4,200 workers on the grounds that they were "serving the interests of the Cali Cartel".

The brothers pleaded guilty in exchange of U.S. agreeing not to bring any charges against their family members. Both were sentenced to 30 years in prison. Their lawyers, David Oscar Markus and Roy Kahn, were able to obtain immunity for 29 family members. Gilberto Rodríguez Orejuela is serving his 30-year sentence at the Federal Correctional Institution, Butner, a medium-security facility in North Carolina with a release date of 9 February 2030, when he would be 90 years old.

After 2012, cultivation of coca in Colombia increased to unprecedented levels. When the Colombian government agreed to extradite Miguel and Gilberto Rodriguez-Orejuela to Miami to face charges that they ran the largest cocaine cartel in the world, they did so with the understanding that the brothers would not be tried for acts committed before 1997. That was in keeping with the Colombian government's extradition treaty with the U.S.

Today, Colombia's cocaine trade is not dominated by large cartels, but by a fragmented constellation of armed and criminal groups. These include fronts of the ELN guerrillas; the Gulf Clan neo-paramilitary group; several FARC dissident groups; several regional criminal organizations; small, generally low profile Colombian organized crime structures; and representatives of Brazilian, Mexican, and Venezuelan criminal trafficking organizations. These groups frequently confront each other, but often they also co-operate. Once cocaine leaves Colombian territory, it is much less likely to be trafficked by Colombians than was the case 20 or 25 years ago.

Queenpin Griselda Blanco – La Madrina or the Godmother

Almost all the top leaders or "kingpins" in the drug trade have been men. One of the most ruthless drug "Queenpins" of all time was Griselda Blanco, nicknamed "La Madrina," or "The Godmother." Blanco was one of the important figures associated with the Medellín Cartel and a central figure in the violent drug wars in Miami in the 1970s and 1980s. She has been credited with being a mentor to Escobar, who later became her enemy.

Blanco was born in Santa Marta, Colombia on 15 February 1943. She grew up in poverty. Her life of crime began at an early age. According to some accounts, she helped kidnap a boy at the age of 11, and after his wealthy family refused to pay the ransom, she fatally shot him. She was also alleged to be a pickpocket and prostitute. While still a teenager, she married a small-time criminal. The couple had three children. However, subsequently they divorced. Blanco is believed to have ordered her husband's murder several years later.

In the early 1970s, she began a relationship with Alberto Bravo, a drug trafficker whom she ultimately married. It was through Alberto that she became involved in the cocaine trade. With New York City as their base, the couple began smuggling the drug into the U.S. Blanco designed bras and girdles and lingerie specially fabricated to smuggle cocaine. She left Colombia in the early 70s and settled in Queens, New York, where she set up a large-scale operation. In 1975, the government intercepted a huge cocaine shipment and she was indicted.

Blanco fled back to Colombia, but it wasn't long before she returned. This time to Miami. In the 1980s, Blanco painted Miami white and red - white with cocaine and red with the blood of drug rivals. Her favorite method of killing included drive-by shootings via motorcycle. Miami experienced a wave of Blanco-related crime, including a submachine-gun attack at a mall. Blanco's hey days were called the Miami Drug War. During this violence, there was an environment of complete lawlessness and disruption. The law enforcement agencies formed the Central Tactical Unit (CENTAC 26) - a joint operation carried out by the Drug Enforcement Administration Anti-Drug Operation and Miami-Dade Police Department to bring an end to the influx of cocaine into Miami.

Targeted by rivals and fearing for her life, in 1984 Blanco moved to California. However, the following year, she was arrested and taken to New York to face the 1975 drug charges. In 1985, she was found guilty and sentenced to the maximum term of 15 years in prison, though she reportedly continued to run her empire from inside the prison. During this time, officials looked to press additional charges against Blanco, who was implicated in more than 200 murders. In 1998, Blanco ultimately pleaded guilty in exchange for a reduced sentence. She was released six years later and deported to Colombia.

Blanco instigated anywhere between 40 and 250 murders, including a few personal ones (she shot one of her husbands at point-blank range over a drug deal). Eventually, Blanco was imprisoned, but that didn't stop her. From the inside, she plotted to kidnap John F. Kennedy, Jr. in a plan that was foiled only by an insider's betrayal.

Blanco revelled in her "Godmother" status, going as far as naming her youngest son Michael Corleone after the character in The Godfather. However like a character in a movie, she had an ironic and tragic end. In 2012, Blanco was gunned down in front of a butcher's shop in Medellín by an assassin on a motorcycle, murdered by the very same method she had so often used to dispatch her own enemies.

Blanco became one of the world's wealthiest drug traffickers. According to reports, she smuggled more than three tons of cocaine into the U.S. annually - netting some $ 80 million per month. Her legacy was such that she was picturized through the medium of films, books, documentaries, like the other

two drug lords Al Capone and Pablo Escobar.

General Manuel Antonio Noriega and the Panama connection

The U.S. had long-standing relationship with General Manuel Antonio Noriega of Panama. General Noriega served as a U.S. intelligence resource person and paid informer of the Central Intelligence Agency (CIA) from 1967, including the period when George Herbert Walker Bush was head of the CIA (1976–77). In the mid-1980s, relations between General Noriega and U.S. began to deteriorate. In 1986, U.S. President Ronald Reagan opened negotiations with General Noriega and requested the Panamanian leader to step down after he was publicly exposed in The New York Times by Seymour Hersh, and was later implicated in the Iran-Contra Scandal. Reagan pressurized him with several drug-related indictments in U.S. courts. However, since extradition laws between Panama and the U.S. were weak, General Noriega ignored these threats and did not submit to Reagan's demands. In January 1988, a convicted American Drug smuggler, Stephen M. Kalish told U.S. Senate investigators that he had given millions of dollars in cash as kickbacks to General Noriega, Commander of the Defence Forces of Panama for his help in drug trafficking and money laundering. In 1988, Elliot Abrams and others in the Pentagon began pushing for a U.S. invasion of Panama, but due to Bush's ties with General Noriega through his previous positions in the CIA and the Task Force on Drugs, and their potentially negative impact on Bush's presidential campaign, Reagan refused.

In 1988, U.S. federal grand juries in courts in Miami and Tampa indicted General Noriega on charges of drug-trafficking. The indictment accused him of "turning Panama into a shipping platform for South American cocaine that was destined for the U.S., and allowing drug proceeds to be hidden in Panamanian banks". U.S. invaded Panama on 20 December 1989. Military operations continued for several weeks, mainly against military units of the Panama army. General Noriega remained at large for several days.

But in the face of the massive manhunt and a $1 million reward for his capture, he had few options left. He took refuge in the Vatican diplomatic mission in Panama City where he remained for 10 days. Finally, on 3 January 1990, General Noriega surrendered to the U.S. Military.

In 1992, a U.S. Federal Court convicted General Noriega on charges of cocaine trafficking, racketeering, and money laundering. He received a 40 year sentence, but his jail term was later reduced. General Noriega completed his sentence on 9 September 2007 after having served 17 years in jail.

However, as he had appealed against his extradition to France, where he had been tried in absentia in 1999 and convicted of money laundering and other crimes, he remained in prison. In 2010, the U.S. Supreme Court refused to hear his appeal. In April, General Noriega was extradited to France, where he went on trial in June. The following month, he was convicted and sentenced to seven years in prison. However, in 2011, France agreed to extradite General Noriega to Panama, where he had been tried in absentia and convicted for the murder of political opponents, including the blatant and brutal murder of Hugo Spadafora, a vocal opponent. General Noriega returned to his home country on 11 December 2011, where he began serving three 20-year prison terms.

Legality of the U.S. attack

The U.S. Government invoked self-defense as the legal justification for its invasion of Panama. Several scholars and observers have opined that under international law, the invasion was illegal. According to these experts, the justifications for the invasion given by the U.S. Government were factually baseless. Moreover, even if the justifications had been true, under international law, they did not provide adequate legal justification for the invasion.

Article 2 of the United Nations Charter, a cornerstone of international law, prohibits the use of force by member states to settle disputes except in self-defense or when authorized by the United Nations Security Council.

Articles 18 and 20 of the Charter of the Organization of American States, written in part in reaction to the history of U.S. military interventions in Central America, also explicitly prohibits the use of force by member states: "No state or group of states has the right to intervene, directly or indirectly, for any reason whatever, in the internal affairs of any other state." (Charter of the Organization of American States (OAS), Article 18.). Article 20 of the OAS Charter states that "the territory of a state is inviolable; it may not be the object, even temporarily, of military occupation or of other measures of force taken by another state, directly or indirectly, on any grounds whatever."
U.S. had ratified the UN Charter and the OAS Charter and therefore under the Supremacy Clause of the U.S. Constitution, in the U.S., they are among the highest law of the land. Other international law experts who have examined the legal justification of the U.S. invasion have concluded that the attack on Panama was a "gross violation" of international law.

In the 88th Plenary Meeting held on 29 December 1989, the United Nations General Assembly by resolution No. A/RES/44/240, passed a resolution which strongly deplored the 1989 U.S. armed invasion of Panama. The resolution determined that the U.S. invasion was a "flagrant violation of international law."

A similar resolution which was proposed by the United Nations Security Council was supported by the majority of its member nations but vetoed by U.S., France and UK.

Noriega, 83, died in Hospital Santo Tomás in Panama City on 7 March 2017. He had undergone surgery to remove a benign brain tumor. He had been placed in a medically induced coma after suffering severe brain hemorrhage during the surgery.

Mexican Drug Cartels

Mexico which is en route between Latin American countries and U.S. had its own share of Drug Cartels. In the 1960s and early 1970s, Mexico was primarily a major supplier of marijuana most of which went to the U.S. However, as U.S. efforts in Colombia slowed down the flow of drugs from South America, Mexico emerged as a source of cocaine.

Guadalajara Cartel - Miguel Ángel Félix Gallardo

The birth of most Mexican drug cartels can be traced to former Mexican Judicial Federal Police agent Miguel Ángel Félix Gallardo (born 8 January 1946), commonly referred to by his aliases - El Jefe de Jefes ("The Boss of Bosses") and El Padrino ("The Godfather"). Félix Gallardo was one of the founders of the Guadalajara Cartel in the 1970s. Throughout the 1970s and 1980s, he controlled most of the illegal drug trade in Mexico and the trafficking corridors across the Mexico – U.S. border along with Juan García Ábrego. He started off by smuggling marijuana and opium into the U.S., and was the first Mexican drug chief to link up with Colombia's cocaine cartels in the 1980s. There were no other drug cartels in Mexico at that time.

Through his connections, Félix Gallardo became the person at the forefront of the Medellín Cartel, which was run by Pablo Escobar. This was easily accomplished because Félix Gallardo had already established a marijuana trafficking infrastructure that stood ready to serve the Colombian cocaine traffickers.

However, the Guadalajara Cartel suffered a major blow in 1985 when the group's co-founder Rafael Caro Quintero was arrested on 4 April 1985 from his Alajuela, Costa Rica mansion while asleep for the murder of DEA agent Enrique "Kiki" Camarena. Caro Quintero was convicted and sentenced to 40 years for the murder of Camarena and other crimes, and extradited to Mexico.

Caro Quintero was first imprisoned at the Federal Social Readaptation Center No. 1 maximum security prison Almoloya de Juárez, State of Mexico. Even though Caro Quintero was to face a maximum of 199 years in prison, Mexican law during that time did not allow for inmates to serve more than 40 years.

In 2007, Caro Quintero was transferred to another maximum security prison, known as Puente Grande, in the state of Jalisco. In 2010, a federal judge granted him the right to be transferred to another prison in Jalisco.

After a motion by Rosalía Isabel Moreno Ruiz, a state judge and magistrate, the Jalisco state court ruled that Caro Quintero was tried improperly in a federal court for crimes that should have been tried at a state level. When Caro Quintero was given his 40-year sentence in the 1980s, he was convicted for murder (a state crime) and not for drug trafficking (a federal crime). The magistrate ordered Caro Quintero's release after he had served time for other crimes he had committed throughout his reign as leader of the Guadalajara Cartel. In the early hours of 9 August 2013, the Jalisco state court ordered the immediate release of Caro Quintero. By this time, he had served 28 years in prison.

The administration of U.S. President Barack Obama was outraged at the release of Caro Quintero. U.S. Department of Justice said they were "extremely disappointed" with the drug lord's release and they were going to pursue Caro Quintero for pending charges in the U.S. Mexico's Attorney General Jesús Murillo Karam also expressed his concern vis-à-vis the case, stating that he was "worried" about Caro Quintero's release and that he would investigate whether additional charges were pending in Mexico.

On 14 August 2013, after the U.S. Government submitted a petition to the Mexican Government, a federal court granted the Office of the General Prosecutor (Spanish: Procuraduría General de la República, PGR) an arrest warrant against Caro Quintero. Once the Mexican authorities re-arrested Caro Quintero, the U.S. Government had a maximum limit of 60 days to present a

formal extradition request. However, Mexico's Attorney General clarified that even if Caro Quintero was arrested, he could not be extradited to the U.S. for the murder of Camarena, because Mexican law prohibited criminals from being tried for the same crime in another country.

Any way, in order to obtain extradition order of Caro Quintero, the U.S. Government would have to present some other criminal charges and accept that he would not face the death penalty if convicted, because there are no laws for capital punishment in Mexico. After his release from prison on 9 August 2013, Caro Quintero has not been seen in the public

On 7 March 2018, the Mexican military used Black Hawk helicopters to search for Caro Quintero, dropping Marines into the mountain villages of La Noria, Las Juntas, Babunica, and Bamopa, all in the Badiraguato Municipality, but their hunt was unsuccessful.

Caro Quintero was among the 15 most-wanted fugitives of Interpol. He was arrested in the settlement of San Simón, within the Choix Municipality of Sinaloa on 15 July 2022 and later transferred to the maximum security federal prison Federal Social Readaptation Center No. 1, also known as the "Altiplano" (in Mexico). He is believed to be 70 year old.

Meanwhile, Félix Gallardo who had actually ordered the murder of Drug Enforcement Administration (DEA) agent Enrique "Kiki" Camarena kept a low profile. In 1987, he moved with his family to Guadalajara. He was arrested in Mexico on 8 April 1989 and charged by the authorities in Mexico and U.S. with the kidnapping and murder of DEA agent Enrique Camarena, as well as racketeering, drug smuggling, and multiple violent crimes.

Division of territory

After his arrest, Félix Gallardo decided to split up the trade as it would be more efficient and less likely to be brought down in one law enforcement swoop. He instructed his lawyer to convene a meeting of the nation's top drug narcos in 1989 at a house in the resort of Acapulco where he demarcated the plazas or territories. The Tijuana route would go to his nephews, the Arellano Felix brothers. The Ciudad Juárez route would go to the Carrillo Fuentes family. Miguel Caro Quintero would run the Sonora corridor. Joaquín Guzmán Loera and Héctor Luis Palma Salazar would take over the Pacific coast operations, with Ismael Zambada García joining them soon after and thus becoming the Sinaloa Cartel. The control of the Matamoros, Tamaulipas corridor - then becoming the Gulf Cartel - would be left undisturbed to its founder Juan García Ábrego, who was not a party to the 1989 pact.

Félix Gallardo who was known as "The Boss of the Bosses" remained one of Mexico's major traffickers. He maintained control over his organization from inside the jail via mobile phones until 1993 when he was transferred to the Altiplano maximum security prison, where he served part of his 37-year sentence. Then he lost remaining control over the other drug lords.

It is believed that the Guadalajara Cartel prospered largely because it enjoyed the protection of the Dirección Federal de Seguridad (DFS), under its Chief Miguel Nazar Haro. Félix Gallardo still planned to oversee national operations.

The Tijuana cartel created by members of the Arellano Félix family, especially the brothers Ramon and Benjamin, which was founded in the late 1980s, became one of the most powerful cartels in Mexico, responsible for shipping hundreds of millions of dollars worth of cocaine, heroin, and meth-amphetamine into the U.S.

However, Tijuana cartel faced fierce, and often violent competition, from other drug organizations, particularly the Juárez, Gulf, and Sinaloa cartels. There were continuous conflicts and disputes amongst the different cartels. All this

led to political, social, and military chaos, and eventually led to the Mexican Drug War, also called Mexico's War against Drugs. Felipe Calderón, from the PAN party, became the President of Mexico on 11 December 2006. He went after the drug lords followed by other succeeding Presidents.

Meanwhile Félix Gallardo, who was in jail, complained that he was living in poor conditions. He complained that he was suffering from vertigo, deafness, loss of one eye and blood circulation problems; that he was living in a 240 × 440 cm (8 x 14 ft) cell, which he was not allowed to leave even to use the recreational area. In March 2013, Félix Gallardo started a legal process to continue his prison sentence at home after he reached his 70th birthday (8 January 2016). On 29 April 2014, a Mexican federal court denied Félix Gallardo's petition for transfer from the maximum-security prison to a medium-security one. However, on 18 December 2014, federal authorities approved his request to transfer him to a medium-security prison in Guadalajara (State of Jalisco), due to his declining health.

On 20 February 2019, a court in Mexico City denied his request to complete the remainder of his sentence in his home. The court stated that Félix Gallardo's defence did not provide them with sufficient evidence to prove that his health issues were putting his life at risk. On 12 September 2022, Felix Gallardo, now 76 years old, was granted house arrest and moved to his home on 13 September 2022.

Sinaloa Cartel - Joaquín "El Chapo" Guzmán

Following the arrest of Gulf Cartel leader Osiel Cárdenas in March 2003, the Sinaloa Cartel began to contest the Gulf Cartel's domination of the coveted southwest Texas corridor. The "Federation" was the result of a 2006 accord between several groups located in the Pacific state of Sinaloa but there were frequent in-fightings. The Sinaloa Cartel was led by Joaquín "El Chapo" Guzmán, who was Mexico's most-wanted drug trafficker with an estimated net worth of U.S. $1 billion. According to the Forbes magazine profile, he was the 1140th richest man in the world and the 55th most powerful.

El Chapo was born and raised in Sinaloa in a poor farming family. He entered the drug trade during his early adulthood through his father, helping him grow marijuana for local dealers. By the late 1970s, El Chapo began working with Héctor Luis Palma Salazar, one of Mexico's rising drug lords. El Chapo helped Salazar map routes to move drugs through Sinaloa and into the U.S. El Chapo later supervised logistics for Félix Gallardo, one of the nation's leading kingpins in the mid 1980s.

Under the leadership of El Chapo meaning "Shorty", because of his short height 168 cm (5 ft 6 in), the Sinaloa Cartel emerged as one of the most powerful drug cartels in the world. It accounted for the majority of illegal drugs in the U.S. and El Chapo became the most powerful drug lord in the world.

El Chapo oversaw operations whereby mass cocaine, methamphetamine, marijuana and heroin were produced and smuggled into and distributed throughout the U.S. and Europe, the world's largest users. He achieved this by pioneering the use of distribution cells and building long-range tunnels near borders, which enabled him to export far more drugs to the U.S. than any other drug trafficker in history.

El Chapo's leadership of the Sinaloa Cartel also brought immense wealth and power. Forbes ranked him as one of the most powerful people in the world between 2009 and 2013, while the Drug Enforcement Administration (DEA) estimated that he matched the influence and wealth of Pablo Escobar.

The Sinaloa Cartel amassed power through murder, bribes, and innovative smuggling techniques, such as the use of tunnels.

El Chapo was first captured on 9 June 1993 in Guatemala and extradited and sentenced to 20 years in prison in Mexico for murder and drug trafficking. He bribed prison guards and escaped from a federal maximum-security prison on 19 January 2001 and resumed command of the Sinaloa Cartel. His status as a fugitive resulted in an $ 8.8 million combined reward from Mexico and the U.S. for information leading to his capture. He was arrested in Mexico on 22 February 2014. But he escaped on 11 July 2015 from the Federal Social Readaption Center No. 1, a maximum-security prison in the State of Mexico, through a tunnel under his jail cell and again resumed command of the Sinaloa Cartel. Mexican authorities recaptured him on 8 January 2016, during a raid on a home in the city of Los Mochis, and extradited him to the U.S. a year later. In 2019, El Chapo was found guilty of a number of criminal charges relating to his leadership of the Sinaloa Cartel. He is currently serving a life sentence at ADX Florence - the nation's most secure supermax prison. According to a 25 October 2021 Reuters report, a lawyer for El Chapo urged the 2nd U.S. Circuit Court of Appeals in Manhattan to overturn the Mexican drug kingpin's conviction, citing juror misconduct and the jail conditions that El Chapo experienced. In January 2022, the Appeals court not only dismissed the appeal and upheld the conviction of El Chapo but also praised the trial judge for his handling of a case that drew international attention.

Emma Coronel Aispuro, 31, El Chapo's wife was arrested at Dulles International Airport on 22 February 2021. She was accused of helping her husband run his cartel and plotting his escape from prison in 2015. She was charged with conspiracy to distribute cocaine, methamphetamine, heroin and marijuana in the U.S. Emma has not been charged with any crimes in Mexico; although her father, Inés Coronel Barreras, and her brother, Édgar Coronel, were arrested on drug charges and allegations of helping El Chapo's first prison escape. Inés Coronel was arrested in 2013 and sentenced to ten years 3 months in prison in 2017. Édgar Coronel Aispuru was arrested in 2015 and is imprisoned in Aguaruto prison, Sinaloa. On 10 June 2021, in a plea bargain deal, Emma pleaded guilty to federal drug trafficking charges in the U.S. District Court for the District of Columbia. On 30 November 2021, Emma was sentenced to three years in prison on charges of drug trafficking and money laundering. She was also to pay $1.5 million in a restitution deal agreed before the hearing. She would be given credit for nine months already spent behind bars since her arrest.

The sentence was less than the relatively light four years requested by the prosecutors, with the judge acknowledging that Emma was only a teenager when she married El Chapo and she readily pleaded guilty after her February 2021 arrest.

Emma is a former beauty queen. In 2019, she had launched a clothing line and appeared on U.S. reality television. Emma and El Chapo have two twin daughters born in 2011. Emma was the last of El Chapo's four wives.

After the arrest of El Chapo, the Sinaloa Cartel is headed by Ismael Zambada García (aka El Mayo) and El Chapo's three sons - Alfredo Guzmán Salazar, Ovidio Guzmán López and Ivan Archivaldo Guzmán Salazar. As of 2022, the Sinaloa Cartel remains Mexico's most dominant drug cartel. And like Al Capone, El Mayo has effectively become Chicago's new Public Enemy No. 1 after the U.S.

State Department tripled the reward for his capture from $5 million to $15 million. El Mayo has never lived in Chicago. And he has never been arrested.

On 24 March 2022, Mario Iglesias-Villegas (37), nicknamed 'Grim Reaper, the former boss of El Chapo's death squad, who was linked to thousands of murders in northern Mexico over a four-year period, was sentenced to life in prison by a Texas judge. Prosecutors say he played a significant role in the deaths of thousands of people from 2008 - 11 in Juarez. He is serving his time in a U.S. prison. He will also fork over a $100,000 fine for his role in the Sinaloa Cartel's operations.

The Gulf Cartel

The Gulf Cartel, a drug cartel originally known as the Matamoros Cartel (Spanish: Cártel de Matamoros), is one of the oldest organized crime groups in Mexico. It is currently based in Matamoros, Tamaulipas, Mexico directly across the U.S. border from Brownsville, Texas. It was founded in the 1930s by Juan Nepomuceno Guerra.

During the Prohibition era, the Gulf Cartel smuggled alcohol and other illegal goods into the U.S. After the end of Prohibition, the criminal group controlled gambling houses, prostitution rings, a car theft network, and other illegal smuggling. It grew significantly in the 1970s under the leadership of kingpin Juan García Ábrego.

Juan García Ábrego era (1980s–1990s)

By the 1980s, Juan García Ábrego began incorporating cocaine into the drug trafficking operations and started to have the upper hand on what is now considered the Gulf Cartel, the greatest criminal group operating in the US-Mexico border.

Juan García Ábrego bargained with the Cali Cartel and settled for 50% of the shipment out of Colombia as payment for delivery, instead of the US $1,500 per kilogram they were previously receiving. This re-negotiation, however, forced Juan Garcia Ábrego to guarantee the arrival of the product from Colombia to its destination.

Juan Garcia Ábrego created warehouses along Mexica's northern border to store hundreds of tons of cocaine. This allowed him to create a new distribution network and increase his political influence. In addition to trafficking drugs, Juan García Ábrego shipped large quantities of cash to be laundered. Around 1994, it was estimated that the Gulf Cartel handled about "one-third of all cocaine shipments" from the Cali Cartel suppliers into the U.S. During the 1990s, the Mexican Attorney General's office estimated that the Gulf Cartel was "worth over US $ 10 billion".

Juan García Ábrego's chain of corruption extended beyond the Mexican government and into the U.S. In 1986, a United States Federal Bureau of Investigation (FBI) agent named Claude de la O, stated in testimony against Juan García Ábrego, that he received over US$ 100,000 in bribes and had leaked information that could have endangered an FBI informant as well as Mexican journalists. In 1989, Claude was removed from the case for unknown reasons, retiring a year later. Juan García Ábrego bribed the agent in an attempt to gather more information on U.S. law enforcement operations.

With the arrest of Juan Antonio Ortiz, one of Juan García Ábrego's traffickers, it became known that between the years 1986 to 1990, the cartel had shipped tons of cocaine in the buses belonging to the United States Immigration and Naturalization Service (INS). As Juan Antonio Ortiz explained, the buses made safe transportation, since they were never stopped at the border.

It also became known that in addition to the INS bus scam, Juan García Ábrego had a "special arrangement" with members of the Texas National Guard who would truck tons of cocaine and marijuana from South Texas to Houston for the cartel.

Juan García Ábrego's business had grown to such length that in 1995, the FBI placed him in the list of the *Top Ten Most Wanted*. He was the first drug trafficker to be on that list. He was captured outside the city of Monterrey, Nuevo León on 14 January 1996 and flown to Mexico City where U.S. federal agent took him in a private plane to Houston, Texas. Wearing slacks and a striped shirt, Juan García Ábrego was immediately extradited to the U.S. where he was interviewed by an FBI agent, and confessed to have "ordered people murdered and tortured," bribed top Mexican officials, and smuggled tons of narcotics into the U.S.

His prosecutors tried Juan García Ábrego as a U.S. citizen because he also had an American birth certificate, although Mexican authorities claimed the certificate was "fraudulent". He also had an official birth certificate that showed Juan García Ábrego was indeed born in Mexico. According to *The Brownsville Herald*, Juan García Ábrego went into the courtroom grinning and talking animatedly with his lawyers who helped him translate his words from Spanish into English language.

After the judge told Juan García Ábrego that he was going to spend the rest of his life in prison, it was clear to everyone that the death penalty was out of the question.

According to the factual documents presented in court on 8 May 1998, from mid-1970s to the mid-1990s, the Gulf Cartel was responsible for trafficking enormous amounts of narcotics into the U.S. Juan García Ábrego was given eleven life sentences in prison. During the four-week trial, 84 witnesses, ranging from "law enforcement officers to convicted drug smugglers," testified that Juan García Ábrego smuggled loads of Colombian cocaine on planes and then stored them in several border cities along the Mexico-U.S. border before smuggling them to the Rio Grande Valley.

Juan García Ábrego was convicted for 22 counts of money laundering, drug possession and drug trafficking. Jurors also ordered the seizure of $ 350 million of Juan García Ábrego's assets - $ 75 million more than what was previously planned.

Juan García Ábrego is currently serving 11 life terms in a maximum security prison in Colorado, U.S. In 1996, it was disclosed that Juan García Ábrego's organization paid millions of dollars in bribes to politicians and law enforcement officers for his protection. After his arrest, it was later proved that the deputy attorney general in charge of Mexico's federal Judicial Police had accumulated more than US$ 9 million for protecting Juan García Ábrego.

Juan García Ábrego's arrest was subject to allegations of corruption. It is believed the Mexican government knew about Juan García

Ábrego's where-abouts all along but had refused to arrest him due to information he possessed about the extent of corruption within the government. It is believed that the arresting officer, a FJP commander, received a bullet-proof Mercury Grand Marquis and US$ 500,000 from a rival cartel for arresting Juan García Ábrego.

After Juan García-Ábrego

The arrest of Juan García Ábrego by Mexican authorities on 14 January 1996 and his subsequent deportation to the U.S. created a power vacuum in the Gulf Cartel and several top members fought for leadership.

Humberto García Ábrego, brother of Juan García Ábrego, tried to take over the leadership of the Gulf Cartel, but failed in his attempt. He did not have the requisite leadership skills nor the support of the Colombian drug suppliers. In addition, he was under observation and was widely known, since his surname meant more of the same. He was to be replaced by Óscar Malherbe de León and Raúl Valladares del Ángel, but they were arrested a short time later, causing several cartel lieutenants to fight for the leadership. Óscar Malherbe tried to bribe officials $ 2 million for his release, but his attempt failed.

Hugo Baldomero Medina Garza, known as *El Señor de los Tráilers* (the lord of the Trailers), was considered one of the most important members in the rearticulation of the Gulf Cartel. He was one of the top officials of the cartel for more than 40 years, trafficking about 20 tons of cocaine to the U.S. every month.

On 17 April 1997, Medina Garza was reportedly shot in the face by gunmen of El Chava Gómez after he had resisted an abduction. The rapid medical treatment saved Medina Garza's life, but he had to retire temporarily from the drug trade. He was interned for two years in Monterrey where he underwent plastic surgery.

Conflict between these two drug traffickers continued until 1999, when El Chava Gómez was assassinated. Having recovered from his surgery in 1999, Medina Garza returned to take control of the Gulf Cartel by directing cocaine shipments coming in from Colombia into southern Tamaulipas, prompting confrontations with another drug lord, Osiel Cárdenas Guillén. By the end of his career, Medina Garza separated from the Gulf Cartel and began to work independently. Medina Garza's luck ended on 1 November 2000 when he was arrested in Tampico, Tamaulipas and imprisoned in La Palma. In November 2004, he was sentenced to 30 years in prison. But in March 2008, a Mexican federal tribunal reduced it to an 11+1/2-year sentence. I think he should be out by now, but there is no news about him.

After Medina Garza's arrest, his cousin Adalberto Garza Dragustinovis was under investigation for allegedly forming part of the Gulf Cartel and for money-laundering. The next in line was Sergio Gómez alias *El Checo*. However, his leadership was short-lived. He was assassinated in April 1996 in Valle Hermoso, Tamaulipas. After this, in July 1999, Osiel Cárdenas Guillén took control of the Gulf Cartel after assassinating Salvador Gómez Herrera alias *El Chava*, co-leader of the Gulf Cartel and his close friend, earning him the name the *Mata Amigos* (Friend Killer).

Osiel Cárdenas Guillén

On 9 November 1999, two U.S. agents from the Drug Enforcement Administration (DEA) and Federal Bureau of Investigation (FBI) were threatened at gunpoint by Osiel Cárdenas and approximately fifteen of his henchmen in Matamoros. The two agents had traveled to Matamoros with an informant to gather intelligence on the operations of the Gulf Cartel. Osiel Cárdenas demanded that the agents and the informant get out of their vehicle, but they refused to obey his orders. The incident escalated as Osiel Cárdenas threatened to kill them if they did not comply with his order and his gunmen prepared to shoot them. The agents tried to reason with Osiel Cárdenas that killing U.S. federal agents would result in a massive manhunt by the U.S. government. Osiel Cárdenas eventually let the two men go, but threatened to kill them if they ever returned to his territory.
This standoff triggered a massive law enforcement effort to crack down on the leadership structure of the Gulf Cartel. Both the Mexican and U.S. governments increased their efforts to apprehend

Osiel Cárdenas. Prior to this standoff, Osiel Cárdenas was regarded as a minor player in the international drug trade. This incident grew his reputation and made him one of the most wanted criminals. The FBI and the DEA filed numerous charges against him and issued a US $2 million bounty for his arrest.

After Osiel Cárdenas took full control of the Gulf Cartel in 1999, confrontations with rival groups heated up. He found himself in a no-holds-barred fight to keep his notorious organization and leadership untouched, and sought out members of the Mexican Army Special Forces to become the military armed-wing of the Gulf Cartel. His goal was to protect himself from rival drug cartels and from the Mexican military, to perform vital functions as the leader of the most powerful drug cartel in Mexico.

Among his first contacts was Arturo Guzmán Decena, an Army lieutenant who was reportedly asked by Osiel Cárdenas to search for and hire the "best men possible". Consequently, Guzmán Decena deserted the Armed Forces and brought more than 30 army deserters to form part of Osiel Cárdenas' new criminal paramilitary wing. They were offered salaries much higher than those of the Mexican Army. These army deserters of the Mexican Army's elite Grupo Aeromóvil de Fuerzas Especiales (GAFE) formed part of the cartel's armed wing *Los Zetas*. These persons served as the hired private mercenary army of the Gulf Cartel.

The creation of Los Zetas brought in a new era of drug trafficking in Mexico. Little did Osiel Cárdenas know that he was creating the most violent drug cartel in the country. Between 2001 and 2008, the organization of the Gulf Cartel and Los Zetas was collectively known as La Compañía (*The Company*).

Among the original defectors were Jaime González Durán, Jesús Enrique Rejón Aguilar, Miguel Treviño Morales, and Heriberto Lazcano, who later became the supreme leader of the independent cartel of Los Zetas.

One of the first missions of Los Zetas was to eradicate Los Chachos, a group of drug traffickers under the orders of the Milenio Cartel, who disputed the drug corridors of Tamaulipas with the Gulf Cartel in 2002. This gang was controlled by Dionisio Román García

Sánchez alias *El Chacho*, who had decided to betray the Gulf Cartel and switch his alliance with the Tijuana Cartel. *El Chacho* was eventually killed by Los Zetas in May 2002.

Osiel Cárdenas consolidated his position and established his supremacy. He expanded the responsibilities of Los Zetas. As years passed, they became much more important for the Gulf Cartel. They began to organize kidnappings; impose taxes, collect debts, and operate protection rackets; control the extortion business; securing cocaine supply and trafficking routes known as *plazas* (zones) and executing its foes, often with grotesque savagery.

In 2002, there were three main divisions of the Gulf Cartel, all ruled by Osiel Cárdenas and led by: Jorge Eduardo "El Coss" Costilla Sanchez, Antonio "Tony Tormenta" Cárdenas Guillen, and Heriberto "El Lazca" Lazcano Lazcano.

Osiel Cárdenas was captured in the city of Matamoros, Tamaulipas on 14 March 2003 in a shootout between the Mexican military and Gulf Cartel gunmen. He was one of the FBI's Ten Most Wanted Fugitives, with a reward of $2 million for his capture. According to government archives, this six-month military operation for his capture was planned and carried out in total secrecy - the only persons in the know were the President Vicente Fox, Secretary of Defense in Mexico, Ricardo Clemente Vega García, and Mexico's Attorney General, Rafael Macedo de la Concha.

Osiel Cárdenas was extradited to the U.S. in 2007. In 2010, he was sentenced to 25 years in prison for money laundering, drug trafficking, homicide, and for having threatened the two U.S. federal agents in 1999. Osiel Cárdenas is currently imprisoned at USP Terre Haute with a release date of 30 August 2024.

Osiel Cárdenas' brother, Antonio Cárdenas Guillén, along with Jorge Eduardo Costilla Sánchez (El Coss), a former policeman, filled in the vacuum left by Osiel Cárdenas and became the leaders of the Gulf Cartel. Antonio Cárdenas was killed in an eight-hour shooting by the Mexican government forces on 5 November 2010. Costilla Sánchez became the co-leader of the Gulf Cartel and head of the Metros, one of the two factions within the Gulf Cartel. Mario Cárdenas Guillén, brother of Osiel and Antonio, became the other faction of Gulf

Cartel and head of the Rojos, the other faction within the Gulf Cartel and the parallel version of the Metros.

The arrest and extradition of Osiel Cárdenas resulted in infighting. Several top lieutenants from both the Gulf Cartel and Los Zetas fought over important drug corridors to the U.S., especially for the cities of Matamoros, Nuevo Laredo, Reynosa and Tampico - all situated in the state of Tamaulipas. They also fought for coastal cities - Acapulco, Guerrero and Cancún, Quintana Roo; the state capital of Monterrey, Nuevo León, and the states

of Veracruz and San Luis Potosí.

After Osiel Cardenas' extradition, through brute violence and intimidation, Heriberto Lazcano, the Chief of Los Zetas, took over control of both Los Zetas and the Gulf Cartel. Lieutenants that were once loyal to Osiel Cárdenas began obeying the commands of Lazcano.

Lazcano tried to reorganize the cartel by appointing several lieutenants to control specific territories. Morales Treviño was appointed to look over Nuevo León; Jorge Eduardo Costilla Sánchez in Matamoros; Héctor Manuel Sauceda Gamboa, nicknamed El Karis, took control of Nuevo Laredo; Gregorio Sauceda Gamboa, known as El Goyo, along with his brother Arturo, took control of the Reynosa plaza; Arturo Basurto Peña, alias El Grande, and Iván Velázquez-Caballero alias El Talibán took control of Quintana Roo and Guerrero; Alberto Sánchez Hinojosa, alias Comandante Castillo, took over Tabasco.

However, there was continuous disagreement between the Gulf Cartel and Los Zetas. Breakup was inevitable. In early 2010, Los Zetas, the Gulf Cartel's enforcers, split from and turned against the Gulf Cartel, sparking a bloody turf war. When the hostilities began, the Gulf Cartel joined forces with its former rivals, the Sinaloa Cartel and La Familia Michoacana, aiming to take out Los Zetas. The Los Zetas allied with the Juárez Cartel, the Beltrán-Leyva Cartel and the Tijuana Cartel.

In response to the rising power of the Gulf Cartel, the rival Sinaloa Cartel established a heavily armed, well-trained enforcer group known as Los Negros. The group operated similar to Los Zetas, but with less complexity and success. There is a group of experts who believe that the Mexican Drug War did not begin in 2006 when the Mexican President Felipe Calderón sent troops to Michoacán to stop the increasing violence, but in 2004 in the border city of Nuevo Laredo, when the Gulf Cartel and Los Zetas fought off the Sinaloa Cartel and Los Negros.

It is believed that while in prison in the U.S., Osiel Cárdenas met Benjamín Arellano Félix, from the Tijuana Cartel. They formed an alliance. Through hand written notes. Osiel Cárdenas gave orders on the movement of drugs along Mexico and to the U.S., approved executions, and signed forms to allow the purchase of police forces. While his brother Antonio Cárdenas Guillén formally led the Gulf Cartel, Osiel Cárdenas made vital orders from La Palma through messages from his lawyers and guards.

Nearly $30 million of the former drug lord's assets were distributed among several Texan law enforcement agencies. In exchange for another life-sentence, Osiel Cárdenas agreed to collaborate with U.S. agents in intelligence information. The U.S. federal court awarded two helicopters owned by Osiel Cárdenas to the Business Development Bank of Canada and the GE Canada Equipment Financing respectively, because both were brought from "drug proceeds".

On 18 August 2013, Mario Ramirez Trevino, an important leader of the Gulf Cartel was captured. He was expatriated to the U.S. in 18 December 2017.

Juárez Cartel (Spanish: Cártel de Juárez) - Amado Carrillo Fuentes
The Juárez Cartel was founded by Pablo Acosta Villarreal in Ciudad Juárez, Chihuahua, across the Mexico-U.S. border around the 1970s. When Pablo Acosta was killed in April 1987 during a cross-border raid by Mexican Federal Police helicopters in the Rio Grande village of Santa Elena, Chihuahua, Rafael Aguilar Guajardo took his place along with Amado Carrillo Fuentes, nephew of Ernesto Fonseca Carrillo.

Amado Fuentes murdered his boss Rafael Aguilar Guajardo in 1993 and seized control of the Juárez Cartel. Amado Fuentes became known as "El Señor de Los Cielos" ("The Lord of the Skies"), because of the large fleet of jets he used to transport drugs. He was also known for laundering money via Colombia, to finance this fleet. He lived discreetly and maintained a low profile. No wild shootouts, no late-night disco hopping. Few pictures of him appeared in newspapers or on television. He was from a new breed, the U.S. Drug Enforcement Administration liked to say, a low-profile kingpin who behaved like a businessman.

Amado Fuentes brought his brothers and later his son into the business. Unfortunately, Amado Fuentes died in July 1997, in a Mexican hospital, after undergoing extensive plastic surgery to change his appearance so that he could enjoy his billions. He should perhaps have moved over to Russia.

In his final days, Amado Fuentes was being tracked by Mexican and U.S. authorities.

The death of Amado Fuentes in 1997 was the beginning of the decline of the power of the Juárez cartel, as Carrillo relied on ties to Mexico's top-ranking drug interdiction officer, division general Jesús Gutiérrez Rebollo.

A brief turf war erupted over the control of the Cartel. Amado Fuentes' brother, Vicente Carrillo Fuentes, commonly known as El Viceroy, became the leader after defeating the Muñoz Talavera brothers.

When Vicente Fuentes took control of the cartel, the organization was in a flux. The death of Amado had created a huge power vacuum in the Mexican underworld. The Carrillo Fuentes brothers became the most powerful organization during the 1990s. Vicente Fuentes was able to avoid direct conflict and increase the strength of the Juárez Cartel. Towards the end of the 1990s and into the 2000s, the relationship between the Carrillo Fuentes clan and the other members of the organization grew unstable. Drug lords from contiguous Mexican states forged an alliance that became known as 'The Golden Triangle Alliance' or 'La Alianza Triángulo de Oro' because of its three-state area of influence: Chihuahua, south of the U.S. state of Texas, Durango and Sinaloa. However, this alliance was broken after the Sinaloa Cartel drug lord, Joaquín "El Chapo"

Guzmán, refused to pay to the Juarez Cartel for the right to use some smuggling routes into the U.S.

Vicente Fuentes then formed a partnership with Juan José Esparragoza Moreno, his brother Rodolfo Carrillo Fuentes, his nephew Vicente Carrillo Leyva, Ricardo Garcia Urquiza; and formed an alliance with other drug lords such as Ismael "Mayo" Zambada in Sinaloa and Baja California, the Beltrán Leyva brothers in Monterrey, and Joaquín "El Chapo" Guzmán in Nayarit, Sinaloa and Tamaulipas.

On 15 July 2010, the Juárez Cartel escalated violence to a new level by using a car bomb to target federal police officers. In September 2011, the Mexican Federal Police reported that the Juárez Cartel was now known as "Nuevo Cartel de Juárez" (New Juárez Cartel). In 2012 it was alleged that the New Juárez Cartel was responsible for recent executions in Ciudad Juárez and Chihuahua.

On 1 September 2013, the Mexican forces arrested Alberto Carrillo Fuentes, alias Betty la Fea ("Ugly Betty"), in the western state of Nayarit. Alberto Fuentes had taken the leadership of the organization in 2013 after his brother Vicente Carrillo Fuentes (fugitive until his arrest in October 2014) retired following a reported illness.

The 58-year-old Vicente Fuentes was one of the U.S. Drug Enforcement Administration's (DEA) most wanted men for whose capture they had offered a reward of $5m (£3.6m). For decades, the DEA and Mexican police had tried to track down Vicente Fuentes. He was arrested in a joint operation by the Mexican Army and Federal Police in Torreón, Coahuila on 9 October 2014. He was then sent to Mexico City and transferred to the federal installations of SEIDO, Mexico's anti-organized crime investigatory agency, where he gave a formal declaration. Two days later, he was formally charged with drug trafficking and organized crime offences. On 14 October 2014, Vicente Fuentes was transferred to the Federal Social Readaptation Center No. 2, a federal maximum-security prison (commonly referred to as "Puente Grande") in Jalisco state.

The Juárez Cartel lost much of its power after the arrest of Vicente Fuentes in 2014. By 2018, the Juárez Cartel's power had declined in its home region of Ciudad Juárez. In June 2020, it was reported that

La Línea was the Juárez Cartel's most powerful faction in Ciudad Juárez. However, by this time, Los Salazar, a powerful cell of the Sinaloa Cartel, had managed to build a significant presence in Ciudad Juárez as well. The Jalisco New Generation Cartel also made its presence in Ciudad Juárez with its New Juarez Cartel, though it failed to deter the hold which La Linea and Los Salazar had over the Ciudad Juárez drug trafficking market as well.

On 14 September 2021, a Mexican court sentenced Vicente Fuentes to 28 years in prison. Juan Pablo Ledezma a.k.a. José Luis Fratello is the alleged current leader of the Mexican gang called La Línea, which is the leading armed wing of the Juárez Cartel and is said to be the current head of the organization.

Joaquín El Chapo Guzman

Joaquín El Chapo Guzman was the leader of the Sinaloa Cartel based in Mexico. He remains one of the most infamous drug lords of the world like Pablo Escobar. El Chapo mostly operated marijuana, cocaine, and methamphetamine. He was also involved in smuggling heroin throughout several regions of the U.S. and Europe who were the world's largest user of the same.

El Chapo was born in Sinaloa on 4 April 1957 - the eldest of seven children - in a poor family in the rural community of La Tuna in Sinaloa state, north-west Mexico. His parents - Emilio Guzmán Bustillos and María Consuelo Loera Pérez - earned their living from farming. His father was officially a cattle rancher but is believed to have been an opium poppy farmer like most farmers of that area. El Chapo was practically illiterate but had high ambitions. "Even as a little child, he had ambitions," his mother told filmmakers in 2014. She recalled he had "a lot of paper money" which he would count and recount.

His first contact with organized crime came at the age of 15, when he cultivated his own marijuana plantation with his cousins. Then, he adopted the nickname "El Chapo" - Mexican slang for "Shorty" (he is only 5ft 6ins, or 1.64m). But his ambitions far exceeded his diminutive stature. In his late teens, Guzmán left La Tuna to seek his fortune in drug smuggling. His mother said, "He always fought for a better life".

El Chapo carried out his trade by means of distribution channels and he constructed tunnels near the borders of the nations. This new method helped him export much larger volumes of drugs compared to what illegal drug traders had earlier carried out.

In 1993, a Roman Catholic cardinal was shot dead in a turf war with rival drug smugglers. El Chapo was among those blamed and a bounty was placed on his head by the Mexican government. His moustachioed face, previously unknown to the public, started appearing in newspapers and on TV screens. Within weeks, he was first arrested on 9 June 1993 by the Guatemalan Army at a hotel near Tapachula, close to the Guatemala–Mexico border. He was extradited and sentenced to 20 years and nine months in prison in Mexico for murder and drug trafficking. He was initially jailed at Federal Social Readaptation Center No. 1. On 22 November 1995, he was transferred to another maximum security prison, Federal Center for Social Rehabilitation No. 2 (also known as "Puente Grande") in Jalisco, He bribed prison guards, lived a lavish life and continued to control the Sinaloa Cartel.

After a ruling by the Supreme Court of Mexico that made extradition between Mexico and the U.S. easier, El Chapo carefully planned his escape. He escaped from the federal maximum-security prison on 19 January 2001. Francisco "El Chito" Camberos Rivera, a prison guard, opened El Chapo's electronically operated cell door, and El Chapo got into a laundry cart that maintenance worker Javier Camberos rolled through several doors and eventually out of the front door. He was then transported in the trunk of a car driven by Camberos out of the town. At a petrol station, Camberos went inside, but when he came back, El Chapo had walked away into the night. According to officials, 78 people have been implicated in his escape plan. Camberos is in prison for his assistance in the escape.

The police say El Chapo carefully masterminded his escape plan, wielding influence over almost everyone in the prison, including the facility's director, who is now in prison for aiding in the escape. One prison guard who came forward to report the situation at the prison disappeared 7 years later, and was presumed to have been killed on the orders of El Chapo. El Chapo allegedly had the prison guards on his payroll, smuggled contraband into the prison and received preferential treatment from the staff. In addition to the prison-employee accomplices, police in Jalisco were paid off to ensure he had at least 24 hours to get out of the state and stay ahead of the military manhunt. The story told to the guards being bribed not to search the laundry cart was that El Chapo was smuggling gold, ostensibly extracted from rock at the inmate workshop, out of the prison. The escape allegedly cost El Chapo $2.5 million. His status as a fugitive resulted in an $8.8 million combined reward from Mexico and the U.S. for information leading to his capture.

El Chapo's cartel became one of the biggest traffickers of drugs to the US. In 2009, he entered the Forbes' list of the world's richest men at number 701, with an estimated worth of $1bn (£709m). He also earned the reputation of being one of the most powerful man of the world.

Following a joint operation by the Mexican Navy, U.S. Marshals Service together with intelligence from the DEA Mexican authorities, El Chapo was arrested on 22 February 2014, around 6.40 AM, from Miramar condominiums, located at #608 on Avenida del Marin, a beachfront area in Mazatlán, He was then flown to Mexico City for formal identification. He was transferred to the Federal Social Readaptation Center No. 1, a maximum-security prison in Almoloya de Juárez, State of Mexico, on a Federal Police Black Hawk helicopter escorted by two Navy helicopters and one from the Mexican Air Force.

On 24 February 2014 the Mexican government formally charged El Chapo for drug trafficking, a process that slowed down his possible extradition to the U.S. The decision to initially file only one charge against him showed that the Mexican government was working on preparing more formal charges against El Chapo, and possibly including the charges he faced before his escape from prison in 2001. El Chapo also faced charges in at least seven U.S. jurisdictions. On 25 February 2014, a Mexican federal judge set the trial in motion for drug-related and organized crime charges. On 4 March 2014, a Mexican federal court issued a formal charge against El Chapo for his involvement in organized crime.

On 11 July 2015, prior to formal sentencing, El Chapo escaped through a tunnel dug by associates into his jail cell in the Federal Social Readaptation Center No. 1. He was last seen by security cameras at 20:52 hours near the shower area in his cell. The shower area was the only part of his cell that was not visible through the security camera.

When the guards did not see him for twenty-five minutes on surveillance video, personnel went looking for him. When they reached his cell, El Chapo was gone. He had escaped through a tunnel leading from the shower area to a house construction site 1.5 km (0.93 mi) away in a Santa Juanita neighborhood. The tunnel lay 10 m (33 ft) deep underground, and El Chapo used a ladder to climb to the bottom. The tunnel was 1.7 m (5 ft 7 in) high and 75 cm (30 in) in width. It was equipped with artificial lights, air ducts, and high-quality construction materials. In addition, a motorcycle was found in the tunnel, which was probably used to transport materials and possibly El Chapo himself.

When the news of the escape broke, Mexican President Peña Nieto was on a state visit in France along with several top officials from his cabinet and many others. Peña Nieto returned to Mexico on 17 July. 2015. In a press conference, Peña Nieto said he was shocked by El Chapo's escape. He promised that the government would carry out an intensive investigation to see if officials had collaborated in the prison break. In addition, he claimed that El Chapo's escape was an "affront" to the Mexican government, and that the government would not spare any resources in trying to recapture him.

Operation Black Swan was a joint U.S. and Mexican-led military operation to recapture El Chapo. On 8 January 2016, following a deadly fire-fight in the city of Los Mochis, Sinaloa, Mexican authorities recaptured El Chapo. During the raid, five gunmen were killed, six others arrested, and one Marine was wounded. The Mexican Navy found two armored cars, eight assault rifles, including two Barrett M82 sniper rifles, two M16 rifles with grenade launchers and a loaded rocket-propelled grenade launcher.

El Chapo was subsequently taken to Los Mochis airport for transport to Mexico City, where he was presented to the press at the Mexico City airport and then flown by a Navy helicopter to the same maximum-security prison from which he had escaped in July 2015.

Mexico government extradited El Chapo to the U.S. on 19 January 2017, a day before Donald Trump took office as U.S. president on vows to tighten border security to halt immigration and drug smuggling. El Chapo was handed over to the custody of HSI and DEA agents

Following a three-month trial, El Chapo was convicted by a federal jury on 12 February 2019 on all 10 counts of the indictment, including narcotics trafficking, using a firearm in furtherance of his drug crimes and participating in a money laundering conspiracy. On 17 February 2019, El Chapo was sentenced by U.S. District Judge Brian M. Cogan to a life term of imprisonment plus 30 years to run consecutive to the life sentence for being a principal leader of a continuing criminal enterprise – the Mexican organized crime syndicate known as the Sinaloa Cartel – a charge that included 26 drug-related violations and one murder conspiracy. The Court also ordered El Chapo to pay $12.6 billion in forfeiture. He was incarcerated in ADX Florence, Colorado, U.S.

On 26 January 2022, 2nd U.S. Circuit Court of Appeals upheld the drug trafficking conviction of El Chapo, rejecting his argument that the jurors improperly followed the case in the media during his trial. The Appeal Court also rejected other arguments made, including jury misconduct and that the conditions he experienced in prison were deplorable, and requesting a new trial.

On 5 June 2022, the Supreme Court of the U.S. rejected the petition of convicted El Chapo without comment. El Chapo is currently serving his imprisonment for a number of criminal charges at an American federal prison.

El Chapo will always be remembered for his escapes through tunnels. According to the reports of the U.S. Drug Enforcement Administration (DEA), tunnels are still used for drug smuggling. One of the recent identification of such tunnels was done by the U.S. Customs and Border Patrol (CBP) which was provided with the name of Tunnel 125 by the U.S. government.

After the arrest of El Chapo, the U.S. government have been able to locate thirty-five passageways which were initially the route followed by El Chapo's Cartel to carry out drug trafficking. The discovered tunnels have proper facilities like elevators, ventilators, steel rails for the carts which were used in order to have a smooth carriage of drugs. Associated with this, the tunnel task force operated by the U.S. Immigration and Customs Enforcement (ICE) in 2018 managed to discover a tunnel that was running from a restaurant in Arizona to that of a house located in San Luis Río Colorado, Sonora and the owner of the restaurant was found to be involved in drug trafficking of well-known drugs like cocaine, methamphetamine, fentanyl. He was arrested right after the investigation. In order to smoothen the procedure of investigating the tunnels, the U.S. Army engineers are working towards designing technology which will help in detecting the tunnels easily.

El Chapo's weakness was his narcissism. He was reaching out to actors and directors to commission screenplays about his life. His communication with actors and producers gifted Mexico's attorney general a new line of investigation.

When he escaped from prison in 2015, he probably could have run away to the mountains and just lived lavishly. Instead, he made the unprecedented move of granting an exclusive interview to Hollywood actor Sean Penn in October 2015. It was a decision that probably cost him his freedom. In the interview published in Rolling Stone magazine, he said, "I have a fleet of submarines, airplanes, trucks and boats,". After his capture, it was speculated - though never formally confirmed - that Mexican authorities found El Chapo by tracking Penn. "He contacted actresses and producers, which was part of one line of investigation," said Mexico's attorney general, Arely Gómez.

Just like Pablo Escobar, El Chapo was also supported by a section of the society for the good works done by him and which are being carried on by his family. These works include helping certain sections of the society where the government had failed significantly. He provided means of living for several depressed classes of people and had also found solutions to the problems associated with different communities of society. Therefore his legacy will be long-lived. And just like Pablo Escobar, he had huge money. During the 11-week trial in New York, Miguel Angel Martinez, a former cartel member told the court that El Chapo was very wealthy, He had homes in every state in Mexico. He had a private zoo, a $10m beach house and yacht he named after himself "Chapito".

In his Rolling Stone interview, El Chapo said it was false to assume drug trafficking would cease "the day I don't exist". Others will soon take his place.

Druglords Of Brazil
Late entrants

The Coca plant is traditionally grown in the Andean highlands of Colombia, Peru and Bolivia. It did not grow in Brazil. Brazil was regarded as a cocaine-consuming nation and was a huge market for the products manufactured in Colombia, Peru and Bolivia. Cocaine produced in these three countries used to enter Brazil through Paraguay which had long served as a transit route for cocaine to Brazil.

Juan Carlos Ramirez Abadia *alias* Chupeta *alias* Lolly Pop

Earlier, leaders like Juan Carlos Ramirez Abadia from Colombia controlled the entire drug business in Brazil. Ramirez Abadia was one of the top leaders of the powerful North Valley Cartel (Norte del Valle Cartel), based near Cali in Colombia. He served time in prison in Colombia from 1996 to 2002 after he had voluntarily surrendered to the authorities. He underwent at least three plastic surgeries to drastically alter his appearance to avoid recognition. Ramirez Abadia was indicted in New York and Washington in 2004 on charges stemming from his leadership of the powerful North Valley Cartel. In a second indictment in 2007 in New York, he was charged with hiring gunmen to kill one of his workers. According to the Washington indictment, between 1990 and 2004, the North Valley Cartel exported more than $10 billion worth of cocaine from Colombia to the U.S.

Ramirez Abadia lived in and operated from Brazil. On 7 August 2007, he was arrested in São Paulo, Brazil, in an exclusive area called Aldeia da Serra. Brazilian authorities found him living luxuriously with his family and running a drug cartel across continents. In March 2008, he was sentenced to 30 years in prison in Brazil. Ramirez Abadia's wife, Yessica Paolo Rojas Morales, was sentenced to 11 years and 6 months in prison for her participation in Ramirez Abadia's operations. Eight other people were also convicted.

Ramirez Abadia had sought extradition to the U. S., saying he feared for his life if he was sent to his home country. Meanwhile, Colombia seized $400 million in property, including a Caribbean island, from the drug lord. They confiscated goods that had belonged to Ramirez Abadia and his wife, including a vintage port and a vast shoe collection. These were sold at an auction in Sao Paulo in April 2008.

On 13 March 2008, the Supreme Federal Court of Brazil granted his extradition to the U.S. He was extradited on 22 August 2008. In 2010, he pleaded guilty to murder and drug charges. As part of a plea deal, he became a witness for the U.S. government in return for a 25 year sentence. He testified at the 2018 trial of the legendary Joaquín "El Chapo" Guzmán, stating that he had been the main supplier of cocaine to El Chapo's Sinaloa Cartel. In May 2022, federal prosecutors acknowledged that Ramirez Abadia had provided useful co-operation and requested his sentencing judge to honour the deal for a sentence of 25 years. Ramirez Abadia was one of the most powerful leaders of Colombia's cocaine cartels. He was considered heir to the dead Colombian kingpin Pablo Escobar.

"His illegal operation included drug manufacturers, couriers, money launderers and accountants, and he and his cohorts resorted to bribery, kidnapping, torture and even murder to further their goal of making as much money as possible," U.S. Attorney Benton Campbell said in a statement.

Coca Plantations in Brazil

In March 2008, Brazil Government authorities discovered the first known coca plantations in Brazil's jungles after satellite images revealed clearings that turned out to be about 2 hectares (5 acres) of coca plantations. Army units in helicopters and small boats also discovered a laboratory to refine cocaine at the site, about 130 kms. south of the border town Tabatinga, along the banks of the Javari river, which runs along Brazil's western border with Peru.

They speculated that the cartels had genetically modified the coca plant to grow in humid jungle conditions. Drug cartels moved into Brazil's Amazon forests and started producing cocaine deep in the rain-forests, opening a new frontier in South America's narcotics trade.

With distribution into the lucrative U.S. market cornered by Mexican cartels, Brazil's gangs trained their sights on Europe. Prices there are higher than in the U.S. due to the longer distances it must travel and the additional risks involved. Europe is also a convenient pit stop for cocaine bound for growing markets in the Middle East and Asia.

Brazil's Drug Gangs

Brazil has three major drug gangs - Red Command, First Capital Command and the Family of the North. These three did not start with drugs. They were formed to fight against the terrible conditions in jails in Brazil.

The Red Command

The Red Command was born out of an alliance between common criminals and leftist militants, when the two groups were thrown together in prisons under the military dictatorship in Brazil from 1964 to 1985. The conditions in Candido Mendes prison, on Ilha Grande island in Rio de Janeiro, were so terrible that the inmates banded together in order to survive within the system. They first formed a left-wing militia organization called the "Falange Vermelho," or "Red Phalanx," but the ideology was soon abandoned and the group became more deeply involved with organized crime, and was dubbed "Red Command" by the press. By 1979, the group had spread out of the prisons and onto Rio's streets. Members on the outside were asked to provide money to those in the inside through criminal activities such as bank robbery, allowing them to maintain a decent quality of life in prison and to finance escape attempts.

When the cocaine trade began to boom in the 1980s, the Red Command was ideally placed to partner with Colombian cartels. It had the structure and the organization to reliably obtain and distribute large quantities of the drug. Members on the outside now had a clear objective - forming well-armed gangs to take over drug turf in the name of the Red Command. They gained control of many poor neighborhoods in Rio de Janeiro that had been neglected by the state, setting up a parallel system of government inside the favelas or shanties and providing employment to inhabitants long excluded from Brazilian society.

By the 1990s, the influence of the city's all-powerful illegal gambling bosses, known as "bicheiros," began to diminish, paving the way for the Red Command to become Rio's top organized crime group and build up its presence in other states.

The Red Command maintained links to the now largely demobilized Revolutionary Armed Forces of Colombia (Fuerzas Armadas Revolucionarias de Colombia - FARC). Red Command leader Luiz Fernando da Costa, alias "Fernandinho Beira-Mar," was arrested in Colombia in 2001 while allegedly exchanging weapons for cocaine with the guerrillas.

In 2005, the Red Command was estimated to control more than half of Rio de Janeiro's most violent areas, though by 2008 this fell to under 40 percent. A police pacification program intended to bring a state presence to criminally dominated areas further reduced the group's influence in the early 2010s, but the security strategy's long-term effects were limited.

At the end of 2016, a breakdown in a longstanding alliance between the Red Command and the First Capital Command (PCC) which was formed in 1993 generated a wave of violence in Brazilian prisons. Over the following year, the conflict between the two groups continued as the PCC sought to reduce the power of the Red Command by forming alliances with enemy gangs as well as co-opting Red Command members with the aim of assuming control over drug trafficking in the group's traditional zones of influence.

The Red Command has a relatively loose leadership structure, and has been described as a network of independent actors, rather than a strict hierarchical organization headed by a single leader. However, there are prominent bosses within the structure, including Luiz Fernando da Costa, alias "Fernandinho Beira-Mar," who is currently imprisoned; and Isaias da Costa Rodrigues, alias "Isaias do Borel," who was in prison for more than 20 years until his release in

2012. In December 2014, authorities in Paraguay arrested a top Red Command leader, Luis Claudio Machado, alias "Marreta."

Fernandinho Beira-Mar has maintained strong influence within the group despite being in jail for life and police have continued to target his legacy. In January 2022, a raid killed Lindomar Gregório de Lucena, alias "Babuino," the Red Command's alleged leader in Rio de Janeiro and Beira-Mar's reported foster son.

On 24 May 2022, Police personnel supported by armed vehicles and a helicopter, attacked the Vila Cruzeiro favela, in a neighborhood of Rio de Janeiro, sparking a ferocious battle in which 23 people were killed. The operation was focused on discovering and apprehending criminal leaders of drug-trafficking group, some of whom were from other states. A woman was accidentally killed after a stray bullet struck her during a gunfight between gang members and the police.

The Red Command is based in Rio de Janeiro, but has a presence in other parts of Brazil, including Sao Paulo. It is particularly strong in the northern state of Amazonas and the western state of Mato Grosso. It also operates in Paraguay and Bolivia. The Red Command worked closely with the PCC, until the two groups' long standing alliance broke down in 2016. While far smaller than the PCC, the Red Command had around 30,000 members around Brazil in 2020.

First Capital Command – PCC

The ideas of the Red Command spread to other prisons. The power of the Red Command also grew. Two decades later, a similar prisoners' movement in São Paulo formed the First Capital Command (Primeiro Comando da Capital – PCC).

Both the Red Command and the PCC organizations were formed by prisoners as self-protection groups in retaliation of Brazil's brutal prison system.

The PCC was formed in the wake of the October 1992 massacre in São Paulo's Carandiru prison, where following a riot, Brazilian security forces killed over 100 prisoners. In August 1993, a group of eight prisoners who had been transferred to Taubaté prison formed the PCC to fight for justice for the massacre and to push for better prison conditions. They expressed solidarity with the older Red Command, adopting its slogan "peace, justice, freedom," and advocated for revolution and destruction of the capitalist system.

The PCC's existence was first publicly reported by journalist Fatima Souza in 1997, but the São Paulo government continued to deny the existence of any such group. In 1999, the group carried out the biggest bank heist in São Paulo's history, stealing some $32 million. In subsequent years, the government split up the PCC's leaders, transferring them to prisons across the country. However, this allowed the gang to forge stronger links with other criminal groups and spread its ideas more widely.

In 1999, a bank robber Marcos Williams Herbas Camacho, known by the nickname Marcola, joined the PCC leadership. Of Bolivian descent, Marcola was considered a genius among criminals. He imposed a new dimension in the organization's business model. By that time, PCC dominated more than two dozen prisons. It also controlled thousands of members free on the streets. The emerging PCC leader understood that at-large members were a precious asset to the organization, useful for increasing revenue, influence, and power.

Under Marcola's management, the PCC began its consolidation as what Max Manwaring called a "second generation gang," organized as much for business as for control of the local terrain. Marcola not only expanded PCC's activity in drug trafficking and bank robbery (the latter was his specialty), he also led the organization to adopt a market view of crime and conquer market share through violence, sweeping away competitors.

By 2001, it had become impossible for the Government to deny PCC's existence, when it coordinated the biggest prison rebellion the world had ever seen. In February 2001, the PCC seized the public attention worldwide when 28,000 inmates took control of 29 prisons in nineteen cities in the state of São Paulo. More than 10,000 people were taken hostage.

In 2006, the PCC launched an even more significant rebellion in protest after the transfer of members to remote facilities. Imprisoned members took over more than 70 prisons across the country, holding visitors hostage. Simultaneously, the group launched coordinated attacks focused on São Paulo that left more than 150 dead.

Over the next decade, the PCC grew in strength and sophistication, aided by a virtually unimpeded ability to conduct business in Brazil's under-resourced prisons as well as a reported truce with the São Paulo police. In the early 2010s, the group began branching out to establish drug and arms trafficking operations in neighboring countries like Bolivia and Paraguay.

In late 2012, São Paulo's public security secretary was forced to resign after a spate of violent clashes between the police and PCC, reportedly in response to authorities ramping up actions against the gang in violation of the spirit of the truce.

During the early 2010s, the PCC also made attempts to influence politics in its home state of São Paulo. With increasing recruitment and revenues, the gang began to emerge as the most powerful criminal organization in Brazil.

With more than 30,000 members across much of Brazil, and with multi-million dollar monthly revenues, the PCC expanded its criminal activities to include large-scale international drug trafficking operations. The group developed ties with the powerful Italian mafia, the 'Ndrangheta, and began laundering money in foreign countries like China.

In the latter half of the decade, the PCC grew bolder and more violent. The group was blamed for a series of armed robberies in Paraguay in 2015. In early 2016, a video surfaced on the internet depicting the decapitation of a teenager, reportedly linked to a dispute between the PCC and its erstwhile ally, the First Catarinense Group (Primeiro Grupo da Catarinense – PGC).

In late 2016, the PCC broke its longstanding truce with the Red Command, setting off months of bloody prison riots that led to hundreds of deaths. Authorities linked the violence to clashes between the two groups over control of lucrative drug trafficking routes running through the remote northern Amazon region of Brazil. PCC was challenging the Red Command in its home city of Rio de Janeiro. PCC was also fending off challenges from a rival group in São Paulo state, contributing to a spike in violence there.

In 2017, the PCC moved into expansion mode. The group linked to international drug shipments travelling through Uruguay, kidnappings and robberies in Bolivia, and attempts to recruit dissident members of the demobilizing Revolutionary Armed Forces of Colombia (Fuerzas Armadas Revolucionarias de Colombia - FARC).

The PCC was also blamed for a spate of murders reportedly linked to conflict over the drug trade in Paraguay. In April 2017, the gang reportedly carried out the biggest armed robbery in Paraguay's history. Between 50 and 60 individuals armed with military-grade weapons and explosives attacked a transportation company just after midnight on 24 April 2017 in Ciudad del Este, a town close to the so-called "Tri-Border" region where Paraguay, Brazil and Argentina meet.

Although the official amount has not been disclosed, according to press reports, around $40 million were stolen. Local media described the operation as "the heist of the century," and described the city as being thrown into a "state of war."

The PCC organizes itself with strong independent local leadership working through a franchise system instead of being dependant on a vertical hierarchy. However, dues are collected from members of the organization and are used to pay lawyers, bribe prison guards and police, and to purchase drugs and weapons. A 2018 report from Brazil's Federal Police described the gang as being run at the highest level by a group of powerful regional leaders, many of whom are incarcerated.

Two founding members of the PCC - Jose Marcio Felicio, alias "Geleião," and César Augusto Roriz da Silva, alias "Cesinha," were expelled from the organization in 2002, and founded a rival organization, the Third Capital Command (Terceiro Comando da Capital - TCC).

According to the Brazilian police, Marcos Willians Herbas Camacho, alias "Marcola," serves as the group's maximum leader, operating from prison where he is serving a two-decade drug trafficking sentence. The group's second-in-command, Abel Pacheco, alias "Vida Loka," is in jail while facing trial for murder charges.

The PCC lost several top leaders in late 2017 and early 2018. High-ranking PCC leader Edison Borges Nogueira, alias "Birosca," was killed in a São Paulo prison in December 2017, after being expelled from the group earlier in the year as a result of a fight between his wife and other prisoners' family members on a bus. Rogério Jeremias de Simone, alias "Gegê do Mangue," allegedly the PCC's third-in-command, and Fabiano Alves de Souza, alias "Paca," another top leader, were killed in February 2018 in a suspected clash with a rival group.

The fallout from the breakdown of the PCC-Red Command truce continued to generate violence in early 2018, with the PCC seemingly undeterred in its ongoing campaign of domestic and international expansion.

The PCC group is now the largest and best-organized criminal organization in Brazil. It is based in São Paulo, Brazil's most populous and economically important state. But it maintains a presence all over the country. In recent years, it has expanded its activities internationally, developing operations in nearly every country in South America in addition to establishing ties with crime groups in Europe and Asia.

In July 2019, Brazilian police arrested Nicola Assisi, reputedly a senior player in Italy's 'Ndrangheta mob, along with his son Patrick, near Santos. They are "accused of being some of the biggest suppliers of cocaine to Europe," They were extradited to Italy. 'Ndrangheta is one of the most powerful mafia type criminal organizationin the world.

Northern Family or The Familia do Norte (FDN)

The Northern Family is the third criminal faction that occupies northern Brazil and some regions in neighbouring countries, such as – Colombia, Peru and Venezuela. It is the 3rd largest faction in Brazil, and the largest in the state of Amazonas. It does not have good relations with other Brazilian factions, having already entered into several faction wars.

The Northern Family was created in 2007 by Fernandes Barbosa, Zé Roberto da Compensa and Gelson Carnaúba (known as Mano G.). It emerged in prisons and outskirts of Manaus, to fight against the precarious and dangerous conditions that existed in prison in Manaus. Between 2015 and 2018, the Northern Family and the Comando Vermelho formed an alliance to prevent the advance of the PCC in Amazonas, generating the War between the PCC and Red Command in 2016. In 2018, the alliance dissolved, generating a confrontation between the Comando Vermelho and Northern Family, weakening the faction.

The Northern Family group had a division in 2017 when a senior member, João Pinto Carioca, alias "João Branco," founded a splinter group, the "Pure Family of the North" (Família do Norte Pura) and the two factions have waged bloody campaigns of violence against each other since then. Particularly violent prison riots between the two groups led to the deaths of 55 inmates between May 26 and 27, 2019.

Videos by FDN members in response to the CV attacks in January 2020 show that what remains of the group is firmly under the command of Zé Roberto da Compensa, with his son, Luciano da Silva Barbosa, alias "L7," emerging as another leader.

Los Caqueteños

Los Caqueteños was founded in 2010 by former members of a local paramilitary force and is based in the Colombian border town of Leticia. According to a Colombian report, it is "the most belligerent organization in the triple frontier region".

In August 2019, the police arrested 19 year old Kevin Valencia Astudillo, head of the network of hitmen belonging to the 'Los Caqueteños. The same year,

a bi-lateral anti-narcotics force attempted to disrupt some of Los Caqueteños' operations around Caballococha. But out in the jungle, the police always appear to be one step behind the traffickers. The mission relied on two aging Russian Mi-17 helicopters provided by the Peruvians. One broke down immediately, causing a delay of a few days while a new part was flown in. Once the chopper was repaired, the mission netted just three arrests. The suspects vanished into the jungle at the sound of approaching aircraft.

The team also torched five so-called paste labs, which perform the first stage of processing on coca plantations. These facilities are typically crude shacks where workers fill plastic barrels with coca leaves, gasoline and other chemicals to form coca paste. This green-hued sludge is then transported to more sophisticated labs to be processed into white, powdery cocaine.

But as the days passed, the paste seizures didn't amount to much. Then came a potential break. An informant said a small plane carrying 300 kilograms (661.4 pounds) of coca paste had crashed during takeoff from a clandestine landing strip. According to the informant there were another 700 kilograms (1,543.2 pounds) by the side of the runway, guarded by 10 heavily armed men.

Around noon the following day, a few dozen Peruvian police set off in the choppers. As the runway came into view, helicopter gunmen strafed it with machine-gun fire. On landing, they found no armed guards, no drugs and no plane. They located the charred wreckage of a Beechcraft Baron 58, a Brazilian-owned aircraft, hacked up and left in the river. It, too, was empty.

A partnership emerged between Brazil's FDN and Los Caqueteños. Shifting gang alliances between different groups at different times add to the complexity.

Port of Santos - State of São Paulo, Brazil

According to its official website, the Port of Santos connects over 600 ports in 125 countries worldwide. It has since been expanded and has earned record profits. It was due to be privatized by the end of 2022. But due to some hiccoughs, the decision has to wait for the time being.

The PCC dominates the nearby port of Santos, which handles some 7,000 containers a day. With Santos swamped with cocaine, port officials have tightened security. Since 2016, every Europe-bound container is being X-ray scanned. In 2019, customs agents nabbed a record 27 tonnes of cocaine at Santos, a 154% increase from three years earlier.

Several criminal organizations are taking advantage of this network. But the PCC, which controls narco-trafficking in São Paulo, is considered one of the most important. PCC has extended its drug trafficking tentacles across the region and has control over several major cocaine trafficking routes, bringing drugs produced in Andean countries into Brazil and moving them to export centers, particularly through ports, such as the Port of Santos.

Between 2010 and 2019, the Brazilian Federal Police (PF) seized a total of 80.7 tons of cocaine at the Port of Santos. In 2020, during the pandemic, authorities seized 14.1 tons of cocaine. In 2021, operations of the Brazilian Revenue Service (RFB, in Portuguese) led to the seizure of some 15 tons of cocaine at the port. According to PF data, about 80 percent of that drug was bound for European countries.

On 3 February 2022, the Brazilian Federal Police found 558 kilograms of cocaine hidden amid packages of coffee beans. The cargo was ready to be shipped from the Port of Santos to Germany. Drug seizures in Brazilian ports, especially Santos, located in São Paulo state and the second largest in Latin America after the port of Colón in Panama, are so frequent that a recent report by the international investigative journalism organization InSight Crime called it "a crucial lynchpin for the global cocaine trade."

In 2015, Belgian customs seized just 293 kilograms (646 pounds) of cocaine hailing from Brazil, less than 2% of that year's haul. The imports have shot up. Belgium has become the top gateway for South American cocaine entering Europe, almost entirely through the port of Antwerp. In 2019, authorities apprehended a record of nearly 62 tonnes of cocaine at Antwerp, Europe's second-largest port. The single-largest share of that - 15.9 tonnes, about a quarter of the total - came from ships arriving from Brazil.

It is a similar story in Spain, Europe's second most important port. Five years ago, Brazil did not rank among the major embarkation points for cargo ships caught bringing cocaine into Spain. The top five slots belonged to Colombia, Venezuela, Portugal, Ecuador and

Chile. Brazil vaulted to the No. 1 spot in 2016 and again in 2018, when law enforcement seized a record 4.3 tonnes from ships arriving from Brazilian ports. Brazil was also the top point of origin for cocaine apprehended entering Germany in 2018, with a historic capture of nearly 2.1 tonnes.

Experts caution that apprehension figures don't tell the whole story. Bigger seizures could also reflect better policing rather than increased flows. But Europe is now "swimming in drugs," and Brazil is playing an increasingly crucial role in getting them there.

According to the United Nations Office on Drugs and Crime (UNODC), Global cocaine production - almost exclusively from Colombia, Peru and Bolivia - more than doubled between 2013 and 2017, to reach an estimated 1,976 tonnes. South America has been awash with high-purity powder in need of buyers. According to the UNODC's World Drug Report 2019, burgeoning supplies have resulted in falling prices that have attracted new users worldwide.

Secco, the Brazilian federal police drug czar, was more circumspect. He said seizures are up because Andean production has risen sharply and more and more cocaine is entering Brazil, "not because of any new investments" in law enforcement.

According to federal police, Brazil's gangs also import cocaine into the remote, northern Amazon region of the country along the so-called triple frontier with Colombia and Peru. They say much of the product enters Brazil by boat along the Amazon River, bound for Manaus, a city of roughly 2 million people. From there, it moves down river until it reaches north-eastern seaports like Suape and Natal in preparation for the Atlantic crossing. Gangs are "less scared and more powerful" than they used to be, said Brazilian Federal Police Officer Charles Nascimento, a veteran of the Amazon drugs beat.

Jair Messias Bolsonaro is a Brazilian politician and retired military officer who has become the 38th president of Brazil since 1 January 2019. Bolsonaro's administration is stepping up anti-narcotics efforts with its Andean neighbors. Bolsonaro's government is hitting at the gangs by targeting their finances and moving jailed leaders to maximum-security federal lockups.

In recent years, Brazil has become one of the major pipeline countries for moving drugs to Europe. This has, in turn, made Paraguay a critical transit station for cocaine smuggled from producing countries, such as Colombia, Peru and Bolivia. Police say the gang bribes or threatens port workers to place cocaine in outbound shipping containers. Some drugs are loaded on cargo ships offshore at sea, with smugglers pulling alongside in smaller craft. The Port of Santos, with its great dynamism, very well developed infrastructure, and thousands of ships circulating weekly, is obviously most convenient for narco trafficking. But the increase in repression and surveillance makes them open or strengthen other routes. There are other well prepared ports in the northeast of the country, such as Recife, Fortaleza, and Salvador, to be able to make this transit to Africa and Europe, mainly through Iberian ports, such as Portugal, Spain via the Canary Islands, or southern Italy and France, which receive this flow via the Atlantic.

Drug Lords Of India

India does not have drug lords and drug cartels to rival those mentioned in the above Chapters. But we do have a very large number of consumers and India may also be a transit country. And the Drug problem is increasing.

According to data from the Narcotics Control Bureau (NCB), the agency responsible for drug law enforcement in India, the total quantity of drugs seized in the country has increased from 23,960 kgs in 2011 to 60,312 kgs in 2020, a growth of 152%. The highest seizures were reported in 2019, with 66,626 kgs of drugs being seized by law enforcement agencies. The data shows that cannabis, heroin, and synthetic drugs like methamphetamine and amphetamines are the most commonly trafficked drugs in the country.

Some of the biggest seizures

1. The September 2018 seizure: The NCB seized 1,000 kg of heroin from a container at the JNPT in Mumbai. The heroin was concealed in a consignment of imported goods and was believed to have originated in Afghanistan. The estimated value of the seizure was around Rs 2,500 crore ($350 million). This was one of the biggest heroin seizures in India's history.

2, The November 2018 seizure: The NCB seized 1,187 kg of cocaine from a container at the JNPT in Mumbai. The cocaine was concealed in a consignment of furniture and was believed to have originated in South America. The estimated value of the seizure was around Rs 2,400 crore ($340 million). This was one of the largest cocaine seizures in India's history.

3. The June 2020 seizure: The Indian Coast Guard intercepted a vessel off the coast of Gujarat and found 1.5 tonnes of heroin, along with other drugs and weapons. The drugs were believed to have originated in Afghanistan and were destined for the international market. The estimated value of the seizure was over Rs 3,500 crore

($500 million). This was one of the largest drug seizures in India's history.

4. The January 2021 seizure: The NCB seized 200 kg of heroin from a container at the Nhava Sheva port in Mumbai. The heroin was concealed in a consignment of talc powder that was being shipped to a foreign country. The estimated value of the seizure was over Rs 1,000 crore ($140 million). This was one of the biggest heroin seizures in recent times.

Country's biggest ever narcotics seizure

Following a tip off, on the morning of 9th May 2019, the Central Industrial Security Force (CISF) intercepted a 31-year-old woman passenger, Nomsa Lutalo, from South Africa, at New Delhi's Indira Gandhi International airport. The woman was to board a flight to Johannesburg via Dubai.

On checking her bags, they found 24.7kg pseudoephedrine in her bags. On questioning, the woman said she had been handed the consignment in Greater Noida by two people from Nigeria. She said she was asked to carry the same to Johannesburg and was promised good money in exchange.

Based on Lutalo's interrogation, an NCB team conducted a raid at the identified premise in Sector P4 of Greater Noida the same day. They found a man, Henry Ideofor (35) and a woman, Chimando Okora (30) living in the house. Both were from Nigeria. During searches, NCB team found several canisters and boxes in the house, containing 1,818kg of pseudoephedrine. They also recovered 1.9kg cocaine. The approximate value of the seized drugs was estimated to be more than Rs1,000 crores. They arrested three persons - two Nigerian nationals and one South African national.

During questioning, Ideofor and Okora told officials they had taken the house on rent and had been living there since 2015. Ideofor and Okora told the officials that they bought the chemical from various illicit sources and were storing it to manufacture drugs. They also used to manufacture fake heroin and illegally transport it out of the country. They claimed to have also distributed the drugs in Delhi-

NCR. The precursor and manufactured drugs were mostly sent to countries in Africa.

This house in Greater Noida was owned by P. N. Pandey, an IPS officer posted with the UP Police's Economic Offences Wing in Lucknow. When contacted by the NCB, Pandey said he had rented out his house through a property dealer and was unaware of the activities going on there. He said, "I had no knowledge of the drug business being run from my house. I have not even received any rent for the past year and have made complaint to the circle officer against the two Nigerian nationals. The rent agreement also clearly mentions that the residents will be responsible for any illegal activity."

The culprits had carefully selected an IPS Officer's house for their illegal activities. It was being used as a drug-manufacturing unit. According to Madhav Singh, Zonal Director, NCB, the seizure is India's biggest-ever narcotics haul and the world's largest pseudoephedrine seizure in the past three years. He elaborated that pseudoephedrine is a precursor used for manufacturing narcotic drugs and psychotropic substances. The export of pseudoephedrine requires a no-objection certificate from the narcotics commissioner.

A new drug - Hydroponic weed

On the basis of prior information, on 19 October 2022, , officers of the Directorate of Revenue Intelligence intercepted and seized two US-origin consignments at the Courier Terminal in Air Cargo Complex, Mumbai. The consignments were declared as 'outdoor concrete firepit'. But they contained about 86.5kg of high-quality hydroponic weed - a new drug (cannabis grown without the use of soil. worth Rs 39.5 crore.

The DRI officers conducted searches at the destination addresses mentioned in the consignments. Follow up searches led the officers to a warehouse and an office linked to the importer. The searches resulted in the crackdown of the drug cartel being run by two Indian nationals in Mumbai. This seizure indicates a new and alarming trend in which hydroponic weed of US-origin is being imported into India.

The biggest seizure of drugs so far

In what is said to be one of the largest ever seizures in the world, on 14 September 2021, authorities seized more than 3,000 kg of heroin - estimated to be worth Rs. 21,000 crore (approximately) - from two containers at Mundra port in Kutch, Gujarat. The containers were initially declared to contain semi-processed talc stones and bituminous coal.

The consignment was smuggled using the maritime route from Kandahar, Afghanistan via Bandar Abbas in Iran. Eight people, including four Afghan nationals, one Uzbek citizen and three Indians had been detained last year.

The goods were imported by Aashi Trading Company located in Vijayawada in Andhra Pradesh. Investigations are still going on.

What about the big fish – international drug syndicates

On 10 February 2023, the Supreme Court remarked that in NDPS cases, small time drug peddlers are mostly caught and not the real culprits who run drug syndicates. Chief Justice of India DY Chandrachud remarked, " We must say that the Government of India and the investigating agencies are not arresting big fish. Why don't you go after international drug syndicates? Try to catch them. You are only catching small fish like agriculturists, someone standing at bus stand or other places."

These seizures are a testimony to the efforts being made by law enforcement agencies in India to combat the drug trafficking problem in the country. But in reality, the seizures represent only a small portion of the amounts actually smuggled, So they also highlight the need for more vigilance and co-operation among law enforcement agencies at the national and international levels to curb the flow of illegal drugs.

Another seizure of Drugs in Kochi

On 13 May 2023, in a joint operation, the Narcotics Control Bureau (NCB) and the Indian Navy, seized – 2,525 kg high-purity methamphetamine, also called crystal meth, valued at 12,000 crore rupees from a vessel in Indian waters.

The seized drugs were in 134 sacks. The methamphetamine was kept in packets of one kilo each.

The mother ship was being stationed at different points in the sea. Smaller boats would go from various countries & collect consignments from the mother ship.

The consignment was meant for Sri Lanka, Maldives and India.

About the Author

Dr Binoy Gupta

The author retired as a top bureaucrat in the Government of India. He holds a Ph.D. in law as well as a large number of post graduate degrees and diplomas. He has authored several books and written hundreds of articles. This book is the result of years of research.

www.ingramcontent.com/pod-product-compliance
Lightning Source LLC
LaVergne TN
LVHW091535070526
838199LV00001B/76